PRAISE FOR IAIN REID AND *ONE BIRD'S CHOICE*

"A laugh-out-loud comic memoir ... What saves the story from being a typical fish-out-of-water tale is Reid's heartfelt look at the foibles of being a family ... Reid finds humour and warmth in unexpected places." — *Maclean's*

"[A]n entertaining memoir that will keep readers engaged and laughing. Reid's writing is both memorable and humbling ... Readers will be glad they have read this book. *One Bird's Choice* is something each generation can relate to."
 — *San Francisco Chronicle*

"Reid's writing is engaging and humorous, particularly in his well-drawn portraits of his parents and a hideous and possessive guinea fowl named Lucius ... Throughout the memoir he examines the ebb and flow of his parents' lives with the eye of a social psychologist." — *Winnipeg Free Press*

"Reid sends [his parents] — and himself — up on virtually every page with gentle but hilarious humour ... It's hard to write humour, and it's not easy to sum it up, either. But Reid might yet be to Lilac Hill what one Stephen Leacock was to Orillia."
 — *Montreal Gazette*

"Reid is a genial narrator... endearing ... a gently funny book."
 — *Vancouver Sun*

"Reid has aptly captured the angst, humour, and quirkiness of his year at home." — *Canadian Press*

ONE BIRD'S CHOICE

A Year in the Life of an Overeducated, Underemployed Twenty-Something Who Moves Back Home

· IAIN REID ·

ANANSI

Hardcover edition first published in 2010 by House of Anansi Press Inc.

This edition published in 2011 by
House of Anansi Press Inc.
110 Spadina Avenue, Suite 801
Toronto, ON, M5V 2K4
Tel. 416-363-4343
Fax 416-363-1017
www.anansi.ca

Distributed in Canada by
HarperCollins Canada Ltd.
1995 Markham Road
Scarborough, ON, M1B 5M8
Toll free tel. 1-800-387-0117

Distributed in the United States by
Publishers Group West
1700 Fourth Street
Berkeley, CA 94710
Toll free tel. 1-800-788-3123

House of Anansi Press is committed to protecting our natural environment. As part of our efforts, the interior of this book is printed on paper that contains 100% post-consumer recycled fibres, is acid-free, and is processed chlorine-free.

15 14 13 12 11   1 2 3 4 5

Library and Archives Canada Cataloguing in Publication

Reid, Iain, 1981–
One bird's choice : a year in the life of an
overeducated, underemployed twenty-something who
moves back home / Iain Reid.

ISBN 978-0-88784-298-6

1. Reid, Iain, 1981–. 2. Adult children living with parents—
Canada—Biography. 3. Adult children—Canada—Biography.
4. Generation Y. 5. Canadian wit and humor (English).
6. Authors, Canadian (English)—21st century—Biography.

I. Title.

HQ755.86.R43 2011   306.874092   C2011-901699-0

Library of Congress Control Number: 2011929944

Cover design: Alysia Shewchuk
Text design and typesetting: Daniel Cullen

Canada Council   Conseil des Arts   ONTARIO ARTS COUNCIL
for the Arts   du Canada   CONSEIL DES ARTS DE L'ONTARIO

*We acknowledge for their financial support of our publishing program
the Canada Council for the Arts, the Ontario Arts Council, and the Government of Canada
through the Canada Book Fund.*

Printed and bound in Canada

To my parents

Contents

If you have any enterprise before you, try it in your old clothes . . .
perhaps we should never procure a new suit, however ragged
or dirty the old, until we have so conducted, so enterprised, or sailed
in some way, that we feel like new men in the old . . .

HENRY DAVID THOREAU, *Walden*

Prologue

THE NEW MILLENNIUM couldn't come soon enough. Not for me anyway. In the year 2000 I turned nineteen, graduated from high school, and enrolled in university. It was also the year I left home. And once I was gone, I was gone. I rarely returned, not even for summers. The taste of independence was too sweet. When my days of study ended, I watched friends pack up and head home to "figure things out." Some did it to avoid the trappings of adulthood, the onset of the daily nine-to-five grind, or just to save money. I couldn't imagine going back to any routine that whiffed of adolescence. Most of our parents left home before their twenties and never looked back. It's only my generation that has adopted a return to the nest as a precondition of adulthood. No, I would find my own way. I vowed that when I left home at nineteen, it was for good. So after four years of university, armed with an unreliable bachelor of arts degree, I headed to Toronto to find work and begin Real Life.

It turned out I wasn't much of a career man, and I often stumbled when answering the inevitable question of what was I up to. "Oh, well, these days, you know, just keeping busy," I would lie, hoping the topic would turn to something less discomfiting, like the weather, religion, or war.

The majority of my friends had dipped a toe into the waters of bright careers and hefty pay stubs. Others were finishing medical school, law school, and postgraduate degrees. I was wearing slippers and mastering the art of stove-top popcorn. Most nights I would make huge batches, loaded with salt and cayenne pepper. I ate a lot of popcorn in those days. I also spent my time writing, mostly for myself and very rarely for money. So I had to find other means to live. It seemed like every few months I was starting a new job, anything to cover food and rent. I even spent some time coaching a basketball clinic at a church. It was at night, for women over forty — women who had never dribbled a basketball before. The job paid forty dollars a week.

My decision to return to my parents' modest farm was made on a whim. I was headed back to Ottawa to prepare and present a weekly book review for CBC Radio. I had pitched the idea, not convinced anyone would accept it. When the morning-show producer in Ottawa emailed saying she liked the idea and wanted to "get started on it by June," I immediately agreed, without a thought as to where I would live. I was thrilled I would be making a bit of money, even a whisper, by finding, reading, and talking about books.

The afternoon I learned that my pitch had been accepted, I met my friend Bob on a Queen Street patio to celebrate. We sat in our hoodies and toques drinking cheap bottles of cold beer. It was a sunny afternoon, but we drank alone because the early spring air was still too chilly for most. And because it was one o'clock on a Tuesday.

"That's brilliant," said Bob when he heard my news. "So where are you gonna stay?"

The book review was temporary, a summer segment, and I was broke, still weighed down by hefty student loans. "I don't really have time to look for a place downtown. I don't know, I guess I'll probably ask my parents if I can stay with them at the farm. I can't see it being for too long."

That was it, the first time I had even considered going back home after almost a decade of living on my own. Neither Bob nor I spoke. We just took long pulls from our beers and stared out onto the crowded street.

That night I called home. I hadn't heard from Mom or Dad in weeks. When I phoned, Mom apologized, telling me they were still lingering at the table, finishing a bottle of wine. "Of course you're welcome back," she announced after I hinted at my plan. "It'll be fun." I was pleased she didn't make a big deal of it. "Guess what?"

"What?" I said.

"No, I'm talking to your father now . . . Guess what?" I could picture Dad sitting across from her at the table, his chair pushed back, wineglass in hand, shrugging his shoulders. "Iain's going to be moving back home for a bit."

"It's only temporary," I reminded her.

"Great," I could hear Dad. "That's great. He's always welcome."

"Do you know when you're going to arrive?" asked Mom.

"No, I'm not sure. Sometime in the next few weeks."

"Well, if you let us know, we can plan something good for supper. Oh, and I'll have to change your bed. You'll be okay in your old room, right?"

"Sure. But don't worry about doing anything like that. I can change the bed when I get home, Mom."

"Does he know when he'll be arriving?" asked Dad.

"No, he's still not sure."

"We could make something nice for dinner, if he knows," continued Dad. "It's getting nice enough to barbecue; we could do steaks maybe."

"Don't you have some of your extra shirts in Iain's closet? You might have to move those out."

"Yes, yes, I'll get them out before he gets home. I think I have a few blazers in there too."

"Seriously, don't go to any trouble. I don't need much closet space. I'll keep out of your way. And don't worry — it won't be for too long."

"I know. We're not worried," Mom said.

"Not worried about what?" asked Dad.

"We're not worried about anything."

"Okay," replied Dad, "but I still don't know what we're not worried about."

"Mom, listen, I better get going." She agreed, saying she had to get started on the dishes anyway. But we chatted aimlessly for another half-hour or so, mostly about the animals on the farm. At one point Dad excused himself to go to the bathroom, declaring his return by asking if he'd missed anything important.

"Okay, well, I guess that's about it. I should get going on those dishes."

"Right. I'll see you soon then, Mom."

"Yup, see you whenever."

In the background I could hear plates being stacked and Dad saying goodbye. "Oh, and your dad says goodbye!"

In less than a week I tied up what few loose ends needed knotting, packed up the contents of my microscopic basement apartment, and headed east down the 401.

Summer

One

Back to the Future

APART FROM THE TRANSPORT TRUCKS, the highway is uncharacteristically roomy. At least it is on my side. Across the grassy ditch, the westward lanes heading to Toronto are jammed. In Oshawa I stop for some gas and a coffee. I linger at the rest stop for longer than I need to, reading the paper and people-watching. Most of the travellers seem to be in a hurry. I finish my coffee and get a second one for the road. Back in the car, an hour or so later, I lose the Toronto-area frequency. I scan compulsively through the static for a while. Nothing. So I abandon the radio entirely. My car has no CD or MP3 player. Apart from the grumbling motor, I'm buckled into a muddy silence. My mind is racing along with the trucks. After almost ten years of living on my own, I'm headed back home . . . to live with my parents.

Another hour or so down the road I pass by Kingston, my home for four years during university. I roll down the window to empty the dregs of my cold coffee. The wind rushing in over my arm and face is both loud and restorative.

So despite the noise and nip of chill, I leave it down. I lean back in the seat and rest my left arm on the ledge. I'm telling myself I shouldn't be too concerned about returning home. It's not the end of the world. It's temporary, only a pit stop. I'll probably be gone again after a couple of weeks, a month or two at most.

I almost hit the new gate when I turn into the lane leading up to my parents' farm. When Titan, their Great Pyrenees sheepdog, started exploring the fields across the road, my parents raised a gate at the end of their gravel driveway. They had told me about it on the phone the other night. Because of Titan's new-found ambition the barrier was built from necessity, but with plenty of reluctance. The idea of a gated lane seemed cold and inhospitable. My parents delighted in surprise visitors and displaced drivers who pulled up to the house with a map spread across the passenger seat. So, in their oxymoronic way, they aimed for a welcoming gate. With the car idling behind me, I walk up to it, unhitch the latch, and swing it open.

I turn back to the car and peer into the cramped back seat. It's carrying all of my worldly belongings: a few CDs, some clothes in a garbage bag, and several boxes of used books. Hanging from the tiny hook above the door is my *pièce de résistance*: a shabby umber suit. The same suit I'm wearing in every photo taken at every formal engagement over the past twelve years, from weddings to parties to funerals. I had bought it hastily before a semi-formal dance in high school, hoping the pockets were deep enough to stash king-sized cans of beer.

"Yeah, sure, the brown one," I told the salesman at

Moore's when he held up the first suit he picked from the sale rack. It was 40 percent off. I would have prolonged my decision making had I known the extensive role the suit would play in my adult life.

I open the rusty car door, lean into the back seat, and grab the worn blazer off the hanger. There is a stain on the left breast pocket. I can't remember from what or from when; it just seemed to appear one day, and I never bothered to get it dry cleaned. I slip on the stained jacket over my hoodie and get back in the car. The gravel crunches and pops like crackers under the tires as I drive slowly up to the house.

The farmhouse itself is more than 160 years old, and it acts every bit its age. Built from thick logs, it's drafty and off-plumb. The never-ending repairs call for Sisyphean resolve. A roofed verandah with a handful of chairs and benches and a swing wraps around the front side of the house. Out back are Mom's flower and vegetable gardens and a sinking stone patio that catches the afternoon sun. I see a new metal roof on Dad's homemade sheep barn, which is next to the chicken coop. Another forty or fifty paces down the hill is the duck pond and beyond that the lilac trees, which are a landmark in these parts.

I was five when we moved here in the mid-1980s. It was a thrilling time — an urban family of five stepping off the stable path of suburbia, away from the small lots, paved driveways, and fenced backyards. My parents decided to move out to the country after a stint in England, where Dad was finishing his Ph.D. We'd rented a small dairy cottage in the middle of a large cattle farm in Oxfordshire. Neither Mom nor Dad had lived on a farm before, but they loved it.

They wanted to find something similar, even if on a much smaller scale, when they returned to Canada.

Our farm isn't the typical industrial spread; my parents aren't professional agriculturists. So instead of the economically sound practice of raising one type of animal or crop, my parents have opted for the opposite approach: a separate handful of many breeds and plants — ducks, turkeys, chickens, sheep, dogs, cats, tomatoes, carrots, peppers, pumpkins, lettuce, and radishes. I'm sure they've spent more money on their collection of beasts and bushes than they've made. As my parents age, the animal population thins, but the diminishing numbers don't lessen their importance in my parents' lives.

We moved in a week before Christmas in 1986. That first week, Mom found a sign in the shed. It was white and had LILAC HILL painted in purple across the front. The strip of land bordering the road is lined by thick lilac bushes, and the neighbours had told my parents they would be in for a treat come May, when the flowers came into bloom. They were right: it was a glorious sight to behold. Dad hung the sign on a pole at the end of the lane that first spring.

Growing up, our chores were nothing like the chores of our friends. Instead of cleaning our rooms, washing dishes, and vacuuming, we had to collect eggs, shovel manure, weed the vegetable gardens, and even load up the lambs, chickens, and turkeys when they were set for slaughter. My parents didn't have enough certified farmer in them to kill the animals themselves, so we would entice, catch, and wrestle the animals into Dad's truck and drive them to another farm to have them butchered. The lambs were always the hardest to collect. They were strong and stubborn. A day later we would collect our fresh meat wrapped in paper. We kept it all in a large box freezer. Every Sunday we would take some meat out for the week and have an extravagant home-grown feast that evening.

Eventually my sister, Jean, my brother, Jimmy, and I all grew up and left home before we turned twenty. Being the youngest, I was the last to leave. My parents, on the other hand, have been living at Lilac Hill for almost a quarter of a century now. They've always said they couldn't imagine living anywhere else.

I park my car beside Dad's truck, collect my bags, and labour onto the porch, arms full. From there I can see into the kitchen. I haven't seen Mom and Dad in months. They're standing under the kitchen's yellow ceiling light, and they look distressed. I knee open the door.

"Hey."

"Oh, well, look who it is," says Mom.

Dad turns to face me as well but is less spirited. "Hey, bud."

There is a plate of shortbread cookies resting on the table. Two comatose cats are dozing underneath. Nat King Cole is crooning quietly from somewhere to my left. I set the box down on the chair beside the door and unzip my hoodie.

The kitchen smells of a mix of roast meat, homemade gravy, and freshly baked cookies. Supper dishes and baking sheets are patiently waiting their turn to be washed on the counter. To my right is the fridge, which doubles as a heavy, humming bulletin board. It's always been covered in high-school-locker-style paraphernalia. Children's drawings, handwritten notes, "interesting" and "inspiring" articles from the newspaper, and postcards wrap the sides and front of the fridge like a paper quilt stitched together by magnets. The majority of the space is covered with photographs of friends, family, and the animals.

I see a picture of Jimmy, me, and two of our boyhood pals. I can't be much older than nine. Jimmy and I are dressed in long trench coats and holding toy machine guns. One of our chums has a toy handgun tucked under his belt, gangster-style. The photograph was taken one Saturday afternoon when we were engaged in a game we called Cops and Dealers. Two would play the role of cop, the other two, drug dealers.

Sometimes Mom would stumble across our little game. Once we had explained the gist of it she would hustle back to the kitchen and fill sandwich bags with flour. "Give these to the dealers," she would instruct, white handprints now covering her shirt. "They should have to hide them somewhere."

"What's that supposed to be?" one of our prepubescent friends would wonder, pointing at the bags.

"Pure coke," Jimmy would snap without missing a beat.

"Straight from Bolivia," I'd add, tucking it into my underwear.

"The good stuff!" Mom would assert.

Two photos above I notice a shot of the ski jump that Jimmy built. He constructed it out of several bales of straw, snow, and ice beside the driveway, close to the big drift. He directed Mom too, sending her to the car and telling her precisely when to floor it. "I shouldn't be doing this," she would say to me on her way outside, wrapping her scarf around her neck, "but he put a lot of effort into that damn jump and it does look fun. But don't tell Dad."

Jimmy would grab a rope he'd fastened to the bumper of the truck, and Mom, as instructed, would floor it. The tires would spin and then they were off. It looked like Jimmy was water skiing down the driveway, but instead of wearing a life jacket, he wore a parka. I would sit inside on the couch, sipping tea and watching for hours as Mom raced down the lane and Jimmy sailed off the jump high into the air. Over and over.

Directly in the middle of the fridge, below a picture of Jean playing her trumpet, is a shot of Lambo. Lambo was a gaunt lamb who ended up living in our kitchen for a few weeks when his mother rejected him. I think it was Dad who dubbed him Lambo. Mom dressed him in an adult diaper to keep the floor manure-free, and bottle-fed him every couple of hours. When the local paper caught wind of the story, they sent their photographer to the farm. Regrettably the picture made the front page of the city section, which consequently made the front of my locker at school the next morning. Most people had stopped calling me Lambo by the end of the year . . . the teachers anyway.

I turn my attention away from the photos and back to my parents. "What's wrong?" I ask. "Why the long faces?"

"It's nothing," answers Mom. "How was your drive home?"

"Nothing?" says Dad. He holds up a tiny metal staple. "I found this in the stuffing."

"I just don't know how it could have happened," Mom says.

"It must have fallen in when you were cooking," reasons Dad.

His shoulders may have lost some width, but even in his sixties Dad's still a large man. At six feet five he towers over my five-foot mom. Dad weighed ninety-three pounds in grade three; Mom was ninety-three pounds on the day they were married. This discrepancy in size is equalled by their clashing personalities. Dad, an English professor and history buff, is a traditionalist, an earnest, paternalistic introvert. Mom is an outgoing people person, a social butterfly with a silly sense of humour who speaks openly from the heart. She's stayed busy over the years doing everything from taking care of infants and small children to running her own catering business, which offered homemade lunches to some of Dad's colleagues. While Dad quotes Blake and Keats, Mom will recite lines from *Peter Pan*. Dad's dress is formal; he likes silk ties and tweed jackets. Mom bought her glasses because they were the "Harry Potter design" and came with a wizard's wand.

They met when they were in their early twenties, at a production of *Shakespeare's Much Ado about Nothing* in Ottawa, where they both grew up. Dad was completing his master's degree in eighteenth-century literature, while Mom was working at a daycare. They exchanged numbers the night they first met and went out a couple of times that summer. By early fall, Mom, looking for an adventure, had decided to buy a used car, quit her steady job at the daycare, and move out west to Vancouver. She lost touch with Dad.

"No, no, I'm sure it was already in the turkey when I stuffed it," Mom's insisting. "How could I miss a staple?"

"Well, I didn't put a sharp piece of metal into the stuffing," says Dad.

"Are you saying I'd put a sharp piece of metal into the stuffing?" asks Mom.

"No, I don't know. I walked by a few times when you were making it; maybe it just fell in."

A year later Mom suffered a horrible crash while riding a motorcycle. She broke her back in three places and her breastbone and spent two months in the hospital. When she was discharged, she flew back to Ottawa so she could continue her recovery at her parents' house.

Dad showed up at the house the first day Mom was back. She was shocked to see him; she hadn't heard from him in months and felt like she hardly knew him — they'd gone out only a couple of times. That night they had a brief visit. Dad asked if he could come again the next day; Mom said okay. Dad visited every night for the next three weeks. Each night he brought a different bottle of wine for them to share. Dad would sit on one of the living room chairs and Mom, still unable to sit up, would lie on her mat on the floor. They would spend the evening sipping wine and chatting.

One night Mom told Dad he wouldn't be able to come over the next night because she was going to a friend's place for supper; it would be her first social outing since the accident. Dad asked how she was getting home. Mom said her friend was going to drive her. Dad suggested she get dropped off at his place, and he would take her the rest of the way. She agreed.

Dad was watching the last game of the 1972 Canada-Russia hockey series with his roommates when Mom was dropped off at his apartment. It was around 1 a.m. when he drove her home. They were lingering outside the house, chatting in his car, when Mom said maybe it was a good thing she was in that accident, otherwise she would still be back in Vancouver.

Dad said, "No, you wouldn't."

Mom said, "What do you mean? Of course I would."

Dad looked at her and said, "Well, what would you say if I asked you to marry me?"

Mom said, "Well, are you just saying 'What would you say if I asked you to marry me?' or are you asking me to marry you?"

He said, "I'm asking you to marry me."

Mom remembers hearing great whoops of excitement from Dad when she accepted. He was jumping up and down in the street, fists in the air, when Mom noticed that he was still wearing his slippers. She remembers saying to him as he helped her out of the car, "No matter how long we're married, I'll never be as feeble as I am now." That was almost forty years ago.

"Why would a staple have fallen off you and into the bird when you walked by?" asks Mom.

"That type of thing happens all the time," asserts Dad. "I'm agreeing it was an accident."

As I watch them pass the sharp piece of metal back and forth between them, I realize it's not their differences that surprise me anymore but their congruencies. Mom's hair, once dark brown, is almost entirely grey; Dad's neatly trimmed silver beard is doing its best to keep up. Their time together has dulled their disparities and amplified their similarities. Each is rubbing off on the other more and more. Maybe one day, like a blanket, they will share only one persona.

"We're just lucky you didn't swallow it," says Mom, holding the staple up towards the light. "It's bloody sharp."

"Yes, we are," says Dad, "and we better not leave it lying around. Now that Iain's home it might happen to him next."

I don't have to look at Dad to know he's serious.

After supper I lug up my stuff to my "new" room. It looks like my bag has vomited a wrinkled heap of clothes onto the floor — I'm less than enthusiastic about unpacking. The posters of now-retired hockey and basketball stars clinging to the walls haven't changed since I was in late elementary school. The commemorative banner of the Toronto Blue Jays' 1993 World Series championship is in the same spot I hung it more than fifteen years ago. Coupled with the Nirvana and Red Hot Chili Peppers posters, I've just stepped back into the early 1990s.

My parents offered up my old bedroom along with Jimmy's and Jean's. Jean's bedroom has also been left mostly intact. It's still full of her books and all the academic and music awards she seemed to win every other month when we were kids. Instead of achievement awards, I collected buttons. My collection is still showcased on a square bulletin board on the wall.

Jimmy's room is the largest, so I did think about taking it. It's been converted into a pseudo guest room. Vacant bookcases line one wall and a tall wooden armoire stands against another. Most of his old stuff is gone; the only traces of his occupancy are a couple of ski poles, his old football pads, and his hockey stick. I decided I wouldn't feel comfortable in there. I'd always be waiting for Jimmy to calmly enter the room, shake his head, and punch me in the nose for lying on his bed.

I walk to the bathroom down the hall and start brushing my teeth. I've been brushing for at least five minutes now. If I stop it means I have to go back to my room. I'm not sure I can face that just yet. I wonder how many of my friends will be falling asleep tonight under the comforting gaze of Joe Carter and Kurt Cobain. How many will whisper goodnight to the painted face of Anthony Kiedis? The excess toothpaste has spilled out from either side of my mouth and onto my chest. I walk over to the window, still brushing.

The moonlight is shining off the barn's metal roof. Living in the city, I'd forgotten how bright the moon and stars are out here. Considering it's late and dark, the visibility is notable. Titan, Lilac Hill's nocturnal chaperone, has clocked in for his shift. I hear his surly bark before I spot him. He must detect something in the far field, a fox or a wolf. I watch from the window as he runs past the barn, setting off the sensor light. It casts a strong glow, lighting up the vegetable garden, the wood shed, even the green hose snaking from the side of the house to the barn. Other than Titan, nothing stirs. Still, he holds his tail high, combatively, like an arched pirate sword.

There's an abrupt knock on the door, followed by Dad's voice.

"You in there, bud?"

"Uh, yes."

"Are you busy?" This time it's Mom's voice.

"Um, not really, just cleaning my teeth."

"We have to show you something," says Dad.

"We don't want to forget," adds Mom.

"Okay, well, do you have to show me now, in the bathroom, or —"

"Yup, in the bathroom," answers Dad.

I open the door. Mom and Dad enter wearing housecoats. It's a small bathroom that's suddenly become much smaller.

"We have to show you something so it doesn't surprise you."

I set my brush down beside the sink; maybe they'll turn, lower their robes in unison, and reveal some elaborate tattoo stretching across their shoulder blades from one back to the other.

"We want to make sure you know how to flush the toilet."

"I'm sorry?"

"The toilet," says Dad, nodding in its direction. "If you don't flush properly it'll just keep running."

"Total waste of our fresh water," says Mom. "And you know we have the best water. It's so clean."

I lean back against the sink, my hands on my hips. "Right, carry on. I'm all ears."

Dad, the teacher in the family, moves into position. He stands judiciously over the toilet. Mom takes a step back, sitting now on the ledge of the bathtub.

"So, when you flush it, like this" — he flushes — "give it a second or two." We stare at the toilet. "Once it starts filling up, just start to jiggle the handle, nice and gentle, just like this." He begins to lightly jostle the handle as if he's tickling the belly of a puppy.

Mom's seen enough. "You don't do it like that for real, do you? That's not how you're supposed to do it."

Dad stops his jostling. He shoots Mom a sullen look. "This is how I always do it."

"But look, the toilet's still running. Here, I usually give it a jolt, like this." She brushes past Dad and shoves down heavily on the plastic handle. "You have to be forceful."

"Watch out you don't break it," says Dad. "That seems awfully reckless."

"It's already broken; that's why you have to be firm," explains Mom.

I would happily leave them here alone, in the dim light of the bathroom, to debate the most proficient flushing technique, be it a light jiggle or a heavy-handed jolt. But I'm still in mid-brush and my mouth is uncomfortably full of foamy toothpaste.

"I think I get the gist of it, guys." I have to keep my head tilted back slightly so as not to lose any more toothpaste. "I'll make sure it's not running."

Somehow my comment has united them again.

"We've heard that before," says Dad.

"Yup, the last time Jimmy stayed over, the toilet ran all night."

"Don't worry, if I get up to pee in the night, I'll jiggle it . . . the handle, I mean."

"Just make sure you wait until you hear the tank stop," says Mom.

"Okay."

They offer their goodnights: a high-five from Mom and a pat on the back from Dad.

"Hey," says Dad, contributing his final point of the tutorial once the bathroom door has closed behind him, "maybe try a little less toothpaste on the old brush next time."

The water is cold, not unpleasantly so, when I splash it onto my chin and chest in handfuls.

The next morning we share a breakfast of freshly laid eggs, buttered toast, fried potato, tomato, and crispy bacon. We talk exclusively of Dad's corduroys. He was thrilled to find them balled up in the back of his closet while looking for a pair of loafers, and immediately put them on. They're wrinkled and frayed at the cuffs. He stands, informing me that these are special cords.

Dad has a vast corduroy collection, so I ask him what distinguishes this pair from all the others. "Easy," he says, "these can be either green or brown, depending on the light."

As I dip a piece of toast into my runny yolk, Dad walks around the kitchen asking Mom if she can detect the colour shift in the changing light. "What about now?" he asks, moving closer to the window, holding one leg out like a ballerina.

"No, dear, they're still brown," answers Mom, with a glass of juice in hand. "Maybe try moving a little towards the fridge. Here." Mom stands, taking Dad's arm, guiding him closer to the fridge.

"Yes, you're right," he says brightly. "Definitely greener over here."

With nothing to add, I decide to leave the two of them to their spirited analysis of Dad's trousers and spend the rest of the morning and early afternoon setting up the space that will become my study. I've picked the wood-panelled room because of its cottagey feel and, more important, its remote locale — location, location, location. The south wall is made up of three large windows that overlook the apple orchard and the two small rock gardens. Whenever I'm not at work, this is where I plan on spending most of my time. Mom and Dad were pleased with the arrangement. Apart from Christmas and the odd celebration, the room sits largely uninhabited. It's filled with mismatched antique furniture my parents inherited from friends and relatives. Mom swears that the old sofa and the ancient tables and chairs give the room a warm, comfy atmosphere, despite the fact that she covers most of it in large white sheets to prevent fading.

Once my computer is set up and my books unpacked, I uncover half of the antique maroon sofa that faces the middle window. If we're able to keep out of each other's way, this might not be so bad. In Toronto I was living in squalor. Each morning I would hop across my grungy kitchen, altering my route to the toaster as I tried to make inroads on the potato bug population. I would use the bugs the same way a frog jumps from lily pad to lily pad, leaving a trail of tiny carcasses smeared into the linoleum.

I'm trying to be optimistic. There are no potato bugs here. It's quiet. There are no busy roads or loud streetcars or bus exhaust or buildings. Just fields and trees. From where I sit I can see the apple orchard, which is home to an assortment of apple trees and bordered at the far end by the thick lilac bushes. I can also see the newest tree on our land. It's about five or six feet from the base of the oldest and tallest apple tree. Dad told me all about it over coffee this morning, before breakfast. He'd planted it only a week before and promises it will flourish in the spot he's picked. He asked me if I'd ever seen a mature magnolia tree in full bloom. "It might take some time," he said, "but once it gets settled it'll have some of the prettiest blooms on the property, all pink and white." It looks dead to me, like a bunch of bare twigs sticking up from the ground.

I grab the first book my hand touches from the pile on my desk and flip through it. John Steinbeck's *The Wayward Bus*. I want to bask in this solitude while I have it. It's short-lived. The sheep have wandered into the orchard. About eight of them, probably the entire flock, are mingling about, nibbling on the long grass. It's the first time I've seen them since I arrived. I'd forgotten how portly and lumpish they are. After a few minutes they notice me too. They remain still, staring unapologetically and chewing their cuds methodically. I turn my attention back to the book but my eyes inadvertently rise above the page, out to the orchard. The sheep are woolly, breathing statues. Again I try and refocus but am unsuccessful. What the hell are they staring at?

I imagine that the sheep are a group of prying tourists. Their guide, our horned ram, named Marshall, is identifying the key sights. I can hear him telling the rest of the drove that he has a special treat for them today. That if they turn their attention to the left they will see one of those human beings inside; maybe they will even recognize him, because he used to live here. Marshall will point out that the bearded man won't be doing much; he will be sitting mostly, breathing. Questions will arise. The ewe with charcoal wool will ask why the human is back. Aren't they supposed to leave this place when they grow up? Aren't they supposed to have a house of their own? *Maybe he's a failure. Isn't it possible he's a failure?* one of the lambs will add. Marshall will nod, telling them they are both likely right.

I've never disrespected our sheep before. As a boy I would stand and rub their ears as they ate their grain. But now I find their infringement on my privacy infuriating. As they continue to gawk, spreading their malicious rumours among the herd, I remain seated but calmly raise my right arm and extend my middle finger. It's an utterly shameful act but it feels good, and I hold the obscenity until my arm starts to tire. The sheep appear unaffected and continue their cud chewing and window gazing.

Perhaps it's the glare of the sun or my focus on the sheep, but I haven't noticed Mom weeding in one of the rock gardens. She's noticed me.

"Okay, okay," she yells, standing with her arms raised defensively, her muddy trowel in hand. "I wasn't even looking in on you. Sheesh!"

She backs away, shaking her head, before I can offer any explanation through the thick pane of glass.

After a supper of grilled chicken and cucumber salad, I'm on the verandah, half lying, half sitting on the swing, watching the sun disappear for another day. I've been alone for about three minutes when Dad appears. He yawns and sits on the wooden chair to my left. I sit up straighter.

"A red sky means it should be another nice day tomorrow," he says.

"I hope it's not too hot."

"So, did you bring your swimming trunks home with you?"

"Uh, I'm not sure. There might be some lying around here." I'm rattled by Dad's question. He's never been much of a swimmer, and regardless of the heat I'm not sure how I feel about a day trip to the public beach with him.

"I only ask because I'm still waiting for a really hot, humid day this summer so I can put on my trunks and clean the barbecue. I mean, really give it a good once-over. You could help me."

I probably should have seen that explanation coming. But I didn't. Now my brow is furrowed. I need to respond appropriately, mask my trepidation while staying noncommittal. "Huh," I sputter, "it could use a cleaning."

Maybe it's my high standards, but the mental portrait of Dad and me in our chlorine-dulled bathing suits, soaping up the outside of the barbecue, hosing each other down when it gets too hot, is somehow not my prototypical summer fantasy.

"And I'm sure Mom would make up a pitcher of that lemonade if we asked her to. You know, the kind she makes with real lemons and club soda."

"Yeah, good stuff," I say, alluding to the refreshing drink. I decide that now's a good time to retire and leave the swing to Dad if he wants it.

The next afternoon the ringing phone pulls me from a dream. Dad has moved one of the new portable phones with call display into my study. Even though I haven't told anyone about my return and have very few friends in Ottawa, he predicts I'll be getting the bulk of the calls. I've been napping on the couch and don't hear him come in. I roll onto my other side and feel the wet drool on the cushion with my cheek. I watch Dad as he bends down to survey the display panel on the phone.

"Uh-oh, it's an unknown number."

"Well, just screen it," I say, squinting at his fuzzy silhouette.

"We can't do that," yells Mom from parts unknown. "We have to answer the phone."

"It's an unknown name too," continues Dad.

"Just let it go to the machine."

"We have to answer it!" screams Mom.

"Go for it," Dad yells back. "You better hurry or the machine will pick up."

"Please, just leave it. I don't feel like talking on —"

I hear the thud of a full laundry basket and Mom's hurried steps racing down the hall.

"Hello," she says, between pants. "Oh, hi, yup, yes. He's right here. *Iain!*"

I take the phone in the other room. When I return, Mom and Dad are sitting on the maroon sofa, sipping tea. Each is holding the mug in both hands. The white sheet from the couch is folded neatly on the floor.

"I tried to tell him *all* the calls were going to be for him, but he didn't believe me," says Dad.

"So, who was it?" asks Mom after I've sat down at my computer, trying to appear busy.

"What do you mean, who was it? You answered it."

"I know, but your dad doesn't know."

"It was Linda." Linda is Mom's friend from down the road.

"*Linda*," says Dad, dramatically. "Why is Linda calling Iain?"

"She heard I was back home and wanted to know if I would ever want to walk Eggroll." Eggroll is Linda's dog. She hasn't been able to walk him recently because of work, and since I "wasn't up to much" she thought it might just be a match. The first and only time I saw Eggroll, he stood a few feet away and growled at me menacingly.

"Oh, that's nice," says Mom. "It would be good exercise for both of you."

"And I bet she'll pay you," remarks Dad.

"She offered me twenty bucks per walk."

"Excellent. It all adds up."

"Anyway, it's just an option to keep in mind," declares Mom.

Something else to keep in mind: I'm in my late twenties, I have no possessions, no money, no savings, and a temporary, low-paying summer job — and I've just moved back in with my parents. And now I'm being offered the chance to walk Linda's temperamental beagle for twenty bucks a pop. Maybe I can also dig up a morning paper route. And while I'm at it, I can pop into Kinko's and print up some flashy orange flyers promoting my babysitting skills to stuff in people's mailboxes.

I take a deep breath and exhale heavily through my nose. I stare at the blinking cursor on the computer screen in front of me. Mom and Dad remain on the maroon sofa, enjoying their tea.

"I'm just thinking out loud, but there are a lot of flies in here this year," says Mom. "And it's a bit dusty. I should come in here and vacuum before you really get settled."

"I haven't noticed the flies as much this year," says Dad, "although I rarely notice houseflies. They don't seem to bother me."

"Yeah, because it's me they always dive-bomb."

"Houseflies don't dive-bomb."

"Cluster flies don't but the houseflies do." As Mom is speaking an errant fly buzzes down from the rafters and momentarily lands on her head before she shoos it away. "You see, you see!"

I stand and, without a word, push the chair back with my legs and lie chest down on the floor like a cadaver.

"I don't know why flies love you. Maybe it's the same reason mosquitoes love me."

"I think it has something to do with the amount of CO_2 we exude."

"What about you, Iain? Do houseflies or mosquitoes seem to land on you more?" asks Dad.

There's something rejuvenating about an unpolluted view in a familiar setting. Lying there, my face turned to the left, I can see the room and its contents in a distinct and refreshing way. Looking under the couch that I normally look at pokes a tiny hole somewhere in my clogged thoughts. I spot a ball of cat fur, a few pieces of straw, and a tiny spider web jutting out on an angle from the wooden leg of a chair. From where they sit, my parents can see only my legs. If I look over my shoulder I can see their socks and slippers. But with their running discourse I don't need to look to know they're still there.

"Oh, I think he's asleep again" whispers Mom.

"On the floor," mumbles Dad. "But you haven't even vacuumed yet."

"I better do that tomorrow; you know how much Iain likes to nap."

They turn their attention back to their tea, until Dad speaks. "What was that?" he asks, startled.

"No, I didn't say anything," answers Mom. "I was just blowing my nose."

Two

One Bird's Choice

I<small>T'S TAKEN ME A FEW WEEKS</small>, but I've finally unpacked most of my stuff. I've been feeling a slight malaise these last couple of days, a tinge of homesickness for Toronto, for the friends I left, the familiar pubs and cafés along Queen Street, the used-book stores and sushi restaurants, the urban parks, the markets, the shows, and the video store where I rented my movies. I'd grown quite fond of Toronto, a world-class city.

Tonight's no different from any other evening at Lilac Hill, the Paris of rural eastern Ontario. I'm hangin' with Ma and Pa at the farm. Mom piles more food onto my plate while interrogating me about my sickly physique. The gleam in her eye tells me she's set herself a personal goal of increasing my body weight by a minimum of ten pounds by the end of the summer. Meanwhile Dad is sharing fashion tips with me. He's left a sweater on my bed to try on. "It still looks brand new," he says. "I honestly think it'll suit you."

Now that I'm back, Dad's fallen into the habit of leaving

me his unwanted old clothes instead of giving them away to Goodwill. Maybe he thinks I need new clothes but can't afford any. My concern isn't strictly our differing styles but, more to the point, our differing sizes. Even though I'm more than six feet tall, Dad's taller and larger. He outweighs me by at least thirty or forty pounds. I'm swimming in most of his shirts and jackets.

I clear my plate and make my way up to my room, flushed and sweaty from Mom's colossal portions. I'm greeted by Dad's discarded sweater lying across my pillow. It's made of black wool and has two yellow stripes running down the front in the shape of a V. I pick it up. It's heavy and smells of dust. I haven't seen it on Dad for more than twenty years. I put it on arms first and let the body fall down over my head. The waist settles at just above my knees and the sleeves cover my hands. I stand in front of the full-length mirror examining my profile.

Holding the bottom of the sweater away from my legs like a wedding gown, I walk over to the window. I can see Mom unclipping laundry from the line. She's not alone. Lucius, their pet guinea fowl, is with her. They are locked in conversation. Every so often Mom stops, bends down, and with her hands on her knees whistles at him. This excites Lucius, who reacts by jumping up and down, flapping his wings, and dancing about, which only encourages Mom to whistle some more. At this rate it will take her another hour or two to get the laundry inside.

I flop down on the bed in my new woollen nightie and glance around the room. The only adornment that's been added since the millennium is my history degree from university. My parents brought it back after the graduation ceremony and had it framed. It's printed in Latin. I can't read Latin. Dad tells me it checks out.

My diploma has proved useful. Not in terms of opening doors or expanding opportunities, but practically speaking. It rests against the foot of my bed, where I've been using it as a rack to dry laundry. It works best for socks and underwear. There are a pair of red boxers and some white tube socks hanging on it right now. They should be ready by morning.

By early the next morning my melancholic spirit has given way to feelings of optimism. Predictably, they're short-lived. I'm scheduled to meet with Laura, the producer at the radio station, at 9 a.m. Laura's been busy and has already rescheduled our meeting twice. Downtown is a forty-five-minute drive from the farm. By 8:15 a.m. I'm alone in the kitchen, finishing the last of my barely edible dry white toast. I found the loaf in the freezer underneath a package of frozen chicken legs. I had to pry each squished piece apart with a knife before I could toast it. I call goodbye to Dad, who's reading the paper in his study.

"Where's Mom?" I ask.

"Mom? She's out with Lucius, giving him breakfast." He says it in a way that makes me feel stupid for even asking.

Few people, apart from the odd ornithologist, would be able to tell you anything practical about guinea fowl. They likely wouldn't know that guinea fowl are native to Africa and generally eat insects and seeds. I bet most are unfamiliar with the average guinea fowl's appearance — how they resemble an unfortunate blend of frumpish partridge and diseased vulture, while their arched posture gives them an unflattering likeness to a stooped chicken. And I'm sure most among us are unaware that guinea fowl are communal birds.

I have the unfair advantage of knowing intimately the physical characteristics and temperament of these creatures. I grew up with the domesticated flock that roamed the fields of Lilac Hill. They were the ideal animal to complement our cast of ducks, turkeys, chickens, dogs, cats, sheep, and bees. Our guinea fowl were the helmeted kind, complete with cranial growths that protruded skyward and resembled bony mohawks. Their tiny heads are the colour of bird droppings and their cheeks are a bright, raw-ground-beef red. They possess physical attributes that only a mother — my mother in particular — could love. After leaving home at nineteen, I rarely gave any thought to our brood of eccentric birds.

Throughout my years at university, care packages would arrive from Lilac Hill that included updates on all of the animals. Tramp, the wise old dog, was starting to limp; Eric, the once burly ram, was eating less; and Cornelius, the rooster . . . well, it turned out that Cornelius was gay. But these detailed descriptions rarely included any mention of the guinea fowl. They were part of the physical landscape of the farm, more like the collection of lilac bushes than livestock. Then one day I received a solemn email from Dad explaining how careless drivers and hungry predators had over the years whittled away our flock, which was now down to two, a father–son duo. For more than a year the pair got along famously and· could often be seen roaming around the meadows and orchard. "They seem happy," Dad wrote, "because they still have each other."

And then one day, unexpectedly, the patriarch keeled over, twitched, and died in front of Dad while he was washing his truck. Our once replete flock of chirping fowl had been diminished to a single lonely bird.

"Now that he's alone he'll probably just wander off," Mom presumed wistfully on the phone one night, as I flipped through a magazine, only half listening. "I just feel bad; after all, they're instinctually communal . . . Maybe he'll bond with the sheep."

Several weeks later, the same night I called about my new job in Ottawa, Mom seemed glad but ultimately preoccupied. She was eager to share her own exciting news. "Oh, Iain, we're just so pleased," she said. "The last guinea fowl has finally settled on his new family. He's not alone anymore."

It took me a second or two to metabolize her statement. "Oh, right, that's great," I said. "So did he settle on the chickens or the ducks?"

"Oh, heavens no," Mom replied, brimming with parental pride. "Neither. He picked us, your dad and me. Lucius could have just wandered off, but he chose us. It's so cute, and he's getting so tame now."

"Lucius?"

"Oh, sure, Lucius. He needed a name, so that's what we've been calling him. Great, eh?"

I concurred and offered my congratulations. When Mom said goodbye and hung up, I stood with the phone dangling in my hand, staring at the wall in my apartment. What exactly was I going home to? I wasn't sure I was ready to accept a new, unfamiliar family member — namely an adopted avian brother named Lucius.

I find Mom sitting on the wooden stoop, breaking off little bits of fresh raisin bread (that I didn't know we had) and tossing them at Lucius's feet. He's happily hopping back and forth, pecking them up at a stunning rate. "Good boy," she's saying. "You love breakfast, don't you? It's the most important meal of the day, even for you."

"Seriously," she says, turning to me, "his appetite's amazing!"

"Right. Well, I'm off to work now, Mom. See you tonight."

"Look, he just loves the raisins. He can isolate them from the bread."

"*Bye.*"

"Okay, right, I forgot, it's your first day. Good luck. I hope you're not in a hurry," she says, still watching the bird intently. "Lucius likes to see us off these days, so it'll take a touch longer to get down the driveway. Cheerio."

By "a touch longer" Mom means it takes an extra ten agonizing minutes to get down the driveway while Lucius pompously struts back and forth across the path of the car every few seconds. "Isn't he funny?" Mom yells from the stoop, doing her own Lucius-like strut. "He's just being affectionate."

I'm not sure what to tell Laura when I arrive for our meeting ten minutes late. Since I don't want to lose this job, blaming traffic seems a better option than laying it at the feet of an overly affectionate fowl.

Apart from my tardy arrival, the meeting goes as expected. Laura explains that the review will fill only about five or ten minutes of airtime each week. I love books, and I love the idea of reading them and then talking about them on the radio. But I'm still unsure about my ability to do so effectively. My brief history in radio isn't exactly glowing.

The first time I'd ever done anything on-air was back in Toronto, where I was working part-time for a popular national radio show at CBC. Most of my duties were limited to replying to emails, completing insignificant paperwork, helping with a few crumbs of audio editing, and putting forth the odd story idea. I didn't feel overly valued. I didn't even have my own computer or desk, let alone my own chair. I was the rear left mud flap: useful in principle but not in any way propelling the car forward. So I was also pitching ideas to other shows, trying to gain extra writing and producing experience. My first piece on the radio was about long-lasting marriages. I interviewed three couples who'd been married for more than sixty years and wrote a script that was broadcast nationally. The couples were great. I was not.

The day I recorded my voice-over for the piece, I sat alone in a dark studio in Toronto while the producer I was working with coached me over the phone from Winnipeg. After recording the script a handful of times, the producer asked if I was tired. "Not really," I told her. She asked if I'd had any coffee yet. I told her, "Yes, a couple of cups." She suggested diplomatically that I get another. She was happy to wait. "I think you just need a bit more, I don't know, life in your voice," she said. We did some more takes. And then several more. It took almost an hour to get a narration that satisfied the producer. The final piece was three minutes long.

A few weeks later I ran into the producer of another show in the cafeteria. I was waiting for a bagel to toast; he was topping up his coffee. "Hey," I said, "coffee's pretty damn good, eh?"

He smiled.

"I have a few ideas for some stories. I was wondering if you guys need any new material these days."

"Sure," he said, stirring a creamer into his coffee with a straw. "We're always looking for fresh ideas."

My idea was to come in and record some humorous anecdotes. I'd written a few based on actual events from my life. One was about the time I tried to throw out my garbage can. It had a crack in it and I didn't want it anymore. I would leave it out at the curb with the rest of my garbage but the collectors never took it. I ended up attaching a note to the unwanted can that said something along the lines of "This is for trash." The note offended the garbage collector; he thought I was trying to be funny.

The other anecdote dealt with dental floss. I'd written about the time I had a piece of popcorn stuck in my teeth and had resorted to my previously unused roll of dental floss to get it out, but in the process a small piece had frayed off between my teeth. It felt much more uncomfortable than the original piece of popcorn, and the rest of the floss was useless against itself.

I know — neither story is very clever or funny, but I needed the extra work. It took a few weeks, maybe a month, but the producer eventually replied, saying I should come to the studio and try recording the pieces. If they turned out, they would air them on the morning show.

Like my first foray into the studio, it took several takes before my voice and delivery were deemed passable. The producer even got me to stand up while recording, hoping that it might help. I was nervous and unsteady. He told me they'd let me know before the pieces aired. The first two times they let me know, I set my alarm and got up to listen, only to discover that they had been bumped. The pieces finally aired one morning around 5:43 a.m. — not the time of day typically reserved for premium content.

I feel that this opportunity in Ottawa, my own weekly on-air book review, shouldn't be wasted. I have to make the most of it. There's no reason to be self-conscious or neurotic; I just have to talk intelligently about books on the radio. I have to sound shrewd, seasoned, and engaged, not like Woody Allen's blundering nephew.

Laura walks me out after our brief meeting. We've agreed to meet again tomorrow at the same time to discuss some of the books I'm hoping to review. Her eyes light up when we reach the front door. She wonders if I want to record any audio from the bookstores I visit; maybe I could interview the owner or other patrons and get some good side stories. She thinks it might add some more substance to the book reviews. I shake her hand and thank her but think it best to stick to the basics. I don't want to bite off more than I can chew.

The next afternoon I'm stuffing my work clothes into the washing machine when Mom appears. The machine's an older model that calls to mind an advancing battle tank as it fills. I have to close the lid to catch her question. She asks for a small favour. They're going to a neighbour's and won't be around for Lucius's dinner.

"Because he's living on the verandah, he's been pooping all over it," she explains. "It's not very appetizing for him to eat dinner around that. So we've been washing it off most nights. Do you think you could do that for us tonight? You don't have any plans, do you?"

By ten after eight I'm imagining my new co-workers sitting in a pub, discussing the day's work and well into their third round of beers, while I, conversely, am standing on the verandah in Dad's rubber boots, glassy-eyed, pressure-washing Lucius's caked feces off the stained floorboards. It's harder than it looks; the dried excrement is determined to stay put. I have to aim the torrent of water on each dropping for several long minutes.

The good news is that I'm not alone. Lucius has generously taken time out of his evening to calmly supervise the entire process like a martinet. His dedication is remarkable. If I squint and bend my head slightly to the left, it looks almost like he's formed his beak into a tiny grin. I look away, out to the fields. A few seconds later I can't stop myself from checking again. The bastard is definitely smiling.

For the rest of the week Lucius continues to demand the majority of my attention. Again, on my next day of work, his inflaming driveway performance results in my being late. Only this time I'm late not for a meeting but for my live on-air spot. I'm lodged in traffic, still about twenty minutes or so from the station, eating a muffin. I'm picking muffin crumbs off the crotch of my pants and popping them into my mouth.

"Coming up after the news, Iain Reid's here, recommending a great summer read."

Fuck.

I barely make it on time and am sweating suitably for someone who's just jogged to the studio from their car three blocks away. My notes are a disorganized paper salad. I feel clumsy and amateurish throughout the review. While stuttering through my description of an Iris Murdoch novel, I brood over Lucius, trying to decide where I stand morally on the issue of killing him. How would I do it? Would I frame one of the other animals? Or just pretend it was an accident, maybe suicide?

"Sorry, Mom," I'd say, holding his limp body by one wing. "It's terrible. I found him floating in the duck pond, beak down. I guess he just couldn't take it anymore . . . bit of a downer, was old Lucius."

The host thanks me and continues on seamlessly, updating listeners on the weather forecast and traffic. I sit in front of the microphone and slip off the headphones. From the other side of the studio, Laura smiles through the glass. It isn't one of those ringing endorsement smiles; it's more of a get-here-on-time-or-we'll-find-someone-else-to-fill-ten-minutes smile. It's becoming clear that my weekly book review is expendable. I'm expendable. I offer a clumsy thumbs-up, gather my notes, and head back to my car.

When I get home, I volunteer to mow a section of the front lawn. The fierce sun is burning my neck and shoulders, negating my energy. It's having the opposite effect on Lucius, who thinks we're playing a game. He ignores me when I explain that the lawn mower is a device designed to cut grass. He believes it's a fun-machine, engineered to provide him pleasure and exhilaration. As I plod forward he prances alongside, pecking at the wheels. Every so often he jumps into the path of the mower and either waits until the last second to flap away or forces me to stop abruptly.

Lucius finally grants me some solitude with only three strips of lawn still to cut. He's found something else, maybe one of the cats or an ant hole, to occupy the remainder of his frenetic afternoon. That is, until I'm on the last strip. I really believed he'd grown bored of our little circus. It was a con. He approaches from behind, so I don't see him until it's too late. I only feel him when he lands on my back, talons first. I jump from shock and fall to the ground, barrel-rolling several times before coming to a rest on my stomach. My heart's pounding. I'm breathing heavily.

"You're a monster!" I yell. A few strands of grass are stuck to my face. Lucius remains beside the mower, hopping from one foot to the other, nibbling on the yellow head of a dandelion.

Later, in bed, I wake to the howls of a pack of coyotes. They're just passing through one of the fields. They generate a lavish, wild sound, giving the impression that fifty or more animals are part of this hysterical group. Dad predicted I'd hear the coyotes if I ever woke up at night. He said they've been visiting a few nights a week this summer. The sound is intense but it doesn't last long, only a minute or two. The commotion fades as they move on to the next field.

I turn onto my side. The coyotes' yelps haven't unnerved me; instead, I'm comforted by a single thought. Maybe tonight Lucius has picked a low branch to roost.

It's a beautifully still, sunny evening, the most pleasant summer night we've had since I've been back. Dad and I have been barbecuing for only a couple of minutes when we're joined by himself.

"Evenin', Lucius," says Dad, taking a sip from his beer. "Going to help us cook, are ya?"

And what a help he is, strutting back and forth, occasionally scratching my sandalled feet with his sharp claws, cawing his disapproval in my direction. I want to remind Dad that too many cooks ruin the broth, but I'm not confident I'll be the one to stay.

As the evening's humidity coats our wineglasses with beads of condensation, we sit reflectively, eating our meal in silence. Not because we don't have anything to say, but because we know better than to compete with Lucius during his twilight serenade. The sound is hard to describe. Imagine, if you can, a deranged farmer plucking each of Lucius's feathers out, one by one, while holding a megaphone in front of his open beak, broadcasting the cries of agony. It sounds something like that. Only louder.

"Oh, sure, he climbs the roof and sings every night," Mom explains. "It's just his little way of letting us know he's going to roost."

During his torturous screeching, any sense of equanimity usually found in the country dusk is violently lost.

"Most guinea fowl are monogamous and mate with one partner for life," Mom continues. I can see my reflection in the window opposite my seat. I'm wearing another of Dad's outcasts: a button-up red plaid number that hangs off me like a flannel blanket. It's hot and particularly unbecoming. "Did you know they were such loyal creatures?"

I don't reply. Instead I roll up the enormous sleeves of my new shirt. I don't want to drag them in the gravy.

Three

Food for Thought

I WAKE UP ON SATURDAY AN HOUR OR TWO earlier than planned. I was hoping for a lie-in. Somewhere off in the distance, the Red Hot Chilli Pipers, a Scottish bagpipe trio, have nudged me awake. Mom and Dad have an extensive album collection. They love music, and it plays constantly from the same weary CD player that sits atop the dishwasher day after day. Its black cord is held in by a frayed piece of duct tape. The music isn't loud, but if you listen for it you can hear it from almost anywhere in the house. It's the Pipers' unconscionable cover of "We Will Rock You" that pushes me past the point of restful sleep. I fling off the covers and swing my legs out of bed. I grab the clock radio off the bookshelf. It reads 8:23 a.m. I set it back down and yawn.

I presented my third book review on the radio yesterday morning. I feel as if it's getting better with each segment. I say "feel" because I don't know for sure. We haven't received any listener feedback. Not one letter, call, or email. I just have to trust my gut.

I stagger downstairs in my shorts and flop down on the couch. It's a sunny morning and the un-air-conditioned house is already feeling warm.

"Oh, I wasn't expecting you up for a while yet," calls Mom from the kitchen over the booming pipes.

"Yeah, I guess I didn't feel much like sleeping in," I say between yawns.

"What about something to eat? We thought we'd wait to see if you had any ideas for breakfast or lunch."

Breakfast or lunch with my parents means two things: a mound of delicious food and a commitment of at least two hours. With my parents you have to take into account the entire process, not just the consuming stage. There is also an extensive planning stage. And with Mom calling out these words to me, the planning stage was set in motion.

"Well," I say, raising myself up on one elbow, "I just woke up and I'm actually not that —"

Before I can finish my thought, Dad's study door creaks open. It's the first sign of him this morning.

I've noticed instances when Dad, standing only a couple of feet away, has asked me to repeat a question two or three times. "Sorry," he'll say, leaning in so close I could reach out and pinch his cheek, "what's that?" And then there are times like Saturday mornings, when provisions are mentioned briefly in passing, and Dad, hidden up to that point, suddenly emerges from his den with the keen hearing of a whitetail deer. "What's this?" he wonders, coffee mug in hand. "Are you guys deciding on breakfast or something?"

Still baggy-eyed, I'm feeling a little overwhelmed from my week of overeating. The smell of rhubarb pie already wafting through the air before 9 a.m. isn't helping.

Since my return home I've discovered that food comes in a steady stream at my parents' house. Like their music, it's always there, flowing along beside you, no matter what time of day. At Lilac Hill, meals aren't just a break to refuel but a comprehensive event designed for pleasure, socializing, and delicious fare.

Mom has trouble telling me to begin, because there's always more on its way. She's like an artist who's unwilling to unveil her latest work, constantly striving for perfection. "Just a second," she'll say, as I pick up my chicken sandwich, open-mouthed, poised to take a bite. "Just let me cut some carrot sticks for you." Or "Wait, that needs a pinch more pepper."

Back in Toronto large meals came along only a couple of times a month, when I took the time to plan them or, on even fewer occasions, was invited out for dinner. Alone, I ate to sustain, often grabbing takeout on my way home or settling for a quick and nutrition-free jar of curry. Lentil and tomato soup, canned chili, tuna, and salmon, frozen tortellini and pizza, bags of regular chips, and frosted cereal were all staples. If I were Irish, grilled cheese would be my potato. Peanut butter never let me down. Neither did the falafel sandwiches at the Lebanese joint down the road; I ate those a few times a month. I would go weeks without eating anything green.

With my parents, however, food of all colours and kinds is unceasingly present: in its most basic form, such as a banana or an apple ripening on the counter; in its most lavishly prepared form, like a homegrown roast turkey with all the trimmings; and, most commonly, in its ethereal form

— food as merely an idea. These days Mom and Dad talk about food more than they eat the stuff, and are constantly Twittering each other throughout the day.

"What kind of day is it, dear?" Dad will ask Mom.

"Doesn't it feel like a homemade mac and cheese day?" she'll reply.

"I'm just gonna go pop up to shower," Dad will verbally tweet Mom (and me by default, because I'm in the same room) as he walks by in his housecoat. Or "I'll just be in my study . . . cleaning my glasses." Later Mom will report, "I just had an idea for a poem; I'm going to go jot it down." They update each other approximately every eight seconds or so. And many of their posts to each other concern food, one way or another.

"Yeah, Iain's finally up," answers Mom for both of us. "He's ready for some lunch."

"Yeah, I figured he would be," says Dad, sitting down across from me. "So what do you feel like?"

"Wait for me," yelps Mom, sprinting in from the kitchen. She sits perched on the arm of Dad's chair like a bird, her right arm resting across his shoulders. There is a white patch of flour just under her left eye. "I've been thinking," she continues. "We haven't had cheese-and-bacon-things-under-the-broiler in a while. They're always good for lunch."

Dad is thoughtful before answering, "Yeah, cheese-and-bacon-things-under-the-broiler are pretty good, but . . . do we feel like lunch stuff or breakfast stuff?"

"Good question," says Mom.

"Because," says Dad, "cheese-and-bacon-things-under-the-broiler are really good for lunch, but I'm not so sure about them for breakfast."

"I suppose you're right, but we could just have lunch," counters Mom.

"Well . . . I guess we could," says Dad, half-heartedly, "but it's just going on for nine. Still a bit early for lunch."

"I could make pancakes. Pancakes are a good breakfasty thing."

"Yup, pancakes are breakfasty."

"And I think we have some sausages in the freezer."

I decide that now is the time to contribute before I'm left in their wake. "Hey, how come you guys call them cheese-and-bacon-things-under-the-broiler?"

"What do you mean?" asks Mom. "That's their name."

"You know," says Dad, "they're those things with bacon and that grated cheese." He pauses momentarily. "Mom puts them under the broiler."

"Yeah, I know what they are, but why do you call them that? You don't call pancakes those flour-eggs-and-milk-things-spooned-into-a-hot-skillet. You call them pancakes."

My question is met by a wall of silence. Finally Dad turns to Mom and whispers loudly, "Sounds like Iain wants pancakes."

"No, that's not . . . It doesn't matter. Why don't we have a few things, like more of a brunch," I offer.

"Well, cheese-and-bacon-things can also be brunchy," says Mom.

"Yeah, that's true," seconds Dad. "But if Iain's dead set on pancakes . . ."

"No, no, I'm really not set on anything. I'm just curious about the system you're running here."

"System? There's no system," says Mom, defensively. "We're just trying to figure this out so we can eat."

Dad is struck by an idea; he sits up straighter in his seat. "We could," he says, holding out his index finger, "we could have a few cheese-and-bacon-things *and* a few pancakes, so Iain's happy."

"So that's really a brunch then," says Mom.

"Well," says Dad, checking his watch again, "I'm still thinking this is more of a breakfast."

"Okay, sounds good, Iain," says Mom, retreating back to the kitchen.

"I'm glad you wanted them," says Dad when we're alone. "Just look out the window — the bright sun, the light breeze. It really is an ideal pancake morning."

After getting through one and a half cheese-and-bacon-things, I'm full. Mom's still hovering over the stove, dropping spoonfuls of dense pancake batter onto the hot pan.

"It's all delicious," Dad's repeating. "We do eat well."

"That we do," maintains Mom. "We certainly do."

"Mmmm, that was great. Thanks guys, but I think I'm going —"

"You still haven't had your pancakes," says Mom. Dad stops eating and peers up from his plate.

"Yeah, it's bizarre — I'm actually a touch full now after the first part of the meal."

"But I made them because you wanted them," Mom says, flipping the two largest pancakes onto my plate directly from the pan.

"That's true," says Dad, nodding in the direction of my crowded plate. "You better have a couple."

As I begrudgingly comply, Dad rests his knife and fork across his plate and links his fingers behind his head. He turns to Mom. "So — any ideas for supper?"

"Hmmm, I'm not sure. Iain, what do you think?"

"Supper," I slur between mouthfuls of pancake, butter, and syrup. "We're not even done breakfast . . . or brunch . . . or whatever it is we're eating."

"Exactly," says Dad, eyes moving back to his watch. "I think it's best if we decide now."

After the meal Dad asks for some help outside. I meet him at the southwest corner of the property, amidst the lilac bushes. He's standing beside the green wheelbarrow.

"What's going on in here?" I ask, ducking under a crooked branch.

"Kindling time."

"Kindling time? You mean kindling for the wood stove?"

"Yup," he answers. "Now's a good time to start collecting while the wood's dry. I usually just take a few hours every now and then. It's not a rush. We should have enough for the winter by mid-September."

Dead branches are scattered throughout the bushes, some barely hanging on to trees, others already on the ground. Dad picks them up one at a time, splitting them into smaller pieces before placing them neatly in the wheelbarrow.

"So, did Mom tell you her friend from yoga heard you on the radio the other morning? She said it was quite interesting."

"Good to know at least one person heard it."

"That's three people. We were still in bed, but we listened too."

"And I thought I'd been aiming a little high hoping for three listeners."

Dad grips the handles of the wheelbarrow, navigating it deeper into the brush. I follow, picking up any dry skinny twigs I see.

My comfort level has increased with the last couple of reviews I've done. I do feel like they're getting better. Still, my weekly summer book review is terminable. It has an expiration date of late August. I knew that going in, so I've been pondering what I should do next.

I break another branch with my foot — one end on the ground, the other held in my hand, and step through the middle. I toss both pieces into the barrow.

I could go back to Toronto. I might even be able to get my job back at CBC. But is that what I want? Maybe I should think about school again. I could always apply to do a master's degree. But that'll probably just sink me deeper into debt.

Dad cracks a branch over his knee as if it were a stalk of celery. "It's funny," he says. "Now that it's just your Mom and me, we use the stove a lot more. We almost ran out of kindling last year. So, come February, you'll be thankful we did this."

"Well, you guys will. I'm sure I'll be back in Toronto by January, Dad." I probably will be. I might be. It's hard to say.

We've kept our pace consistent, far from gruelling but efficient enough that the barrow is starting to fill. It's indicative of many of the chores during summer. Most are mundane and inattentive, such as watering the vegetable garden and repairing broken fences, but crucial to keeping the farm going. It seems as if the bulk of the work during the summer is to prepare for the colder months to come.

It doesn't take the sheep long to join us. It never does when we hang around the orchard. They don't come right into the brush but graze in the field. Our largest sheep is Marshall, the ram. His size and strength are incredible considering that his diet consists of nothing more than grass, hay, and grain. He's built like a football player, all neck and shoulders. He must weigh well over two hundred pounds, maybe even three hundred. His thick horns, curving into two hard points, wrap around each side of his face. He's an impressively built creature. I'm still picking up twigs, but I'm riveted by Marshall.

"Sorry, Dad, but, um, is that right?"

Dad turns his head, peering out towards the sheep, to where I've motioned. "What?"

"Marshall," I say. "Is everything . . . proper?"

"Yeah, that's Marshall. He's great. What about him?"

Marshall's standing only a few feet away now, nibbling at the grass. "It's just that . . . well, those are without a doubt the biggest testicles I've ever seen in my life." It looks like Marshall's using a pink tea towel to hold up two grapefruits between his legs. I'm astounded. The physics of the scene just don't add up.

"He's fine," says Dad, turning back to his haul.

It takes me a moment to steer my focus back to our congregation of twigs. When I do, Dad has once again moved the wheelbarrow ahead. I have to jog to catch up.

My hour or so of fresh air forces me back to the couch. I nap intermittently in the fetal position and wake more tired than before. From where I lie I can see the profile of Mom's lower half; her top half is hidden in the fridge.

I walk into the kitchen, picking at a splinter in my hand. Mom's precariously holding a jar under her armpit while shifting others around in the fridge.

"What's this?" I ask. "Are you hot or something?"

"No, no," she says. "I'm just making room for Dad. He'll be home from the grocery store soon."

"Who called?" I ask.

"What do you mean?"

"There's a message," I say.

Mom and Dad still employ a primordial answering machine with buttons and tapes. The answering machine is larger than the phone. I point out the flashing red light to Mom. She immediately stops what she's doing.

"Oh, right," she says, kicking the fridge door closed. "I hadn't noticed."

There are actually two messages. Both are from Dad, and both are delivered frantically. He's called twice from the soap aisle.

"Hi, guys, it's just me. I'm in the soap aisle." He pauses. "I was hoping you'd answer. I just came across a deal here on some soap, and I know Mom usually likes her Ivory, but this other brand looks okay and is half-price today. And . . . yup, it's a lavender scent. Anyway, I'm thinking of getting the lavender for a change. Maybe I'll try again in a few minutes."

Mom pushes the button for the next message.

"Oh, you're still not there. Or still just not answering. That's a shame. I hope Iain's not convincing you to screen . . . I'm still here. This other soap looks really quite good. Well, I think I'm just going to get it . . ."

"What? No, no! Don't get that other soap. Not the stupid lavender. Get the unscented Ivory!" She yells it like Dad can hear her.

The machine stops and Mom sits down at the table, crestfallen.

"Why don't you call him back? Maybe he's still in the store," I suggest.

"Yes, great idea!" She jumps up and grabs the phone, hurriedly dialling Dad's cell.

She's able to get through as Dad is making his way to the checkout. He has the lavender soap in his cart, but she convinces him to go back and get the Ivory instead.

"That was a close one," she says.

"Yeah," I say. "Way too close."

It's not until Dad returns from the grocery store that I can appreciate Mom's foresight in clearing space in the fridge.

"Can you give me a quick hand with these groceries?" he calls from the door. "I only have a few things."

In his truck I find several brown boxes full of exceptionally large food items. It looks as if he's just stopping en route to aiding in a disaster zone. I pick up the first box in both arms. It's heavier than it looks. I lug it into the kitchen, setting it down on the counter. When I get back with the second box, my arms are sore. Mom's already busy unpacking. Catching my breath, I reach out and grab the first item I see: six glass jars of capers wrapped in cellophane.

"Whoa, what's with all the capers?"

"What do you mean?" asks Dad. "Capers are great."

"Right," I say. "But do we need quite so many?"

"Well, that's how they come at Costco. Don't worry, we'll eat them."

"Wait a sec," I say, picking up another one of Dad's purchases. "Are you guys starting a deli or something?" I'm holding an industrial-size plastic bag full of focaccia buns. It looks like one of those clear garbage bags full of unwanted day-olds that a bakery leaves in the back alley. There must be forty buns inside.

"Wonderful," says Dad, walking back into the kitchen. "You found the buns. Those make the best sandwiches."

"But do we need all of them?" I ask. "It's only the three of us here, isn't it?"

"Well, I got the whole bag for sixteen dollars, so . . ."

I look at the bag again.

"And I'll just freeze what we don't eat," says Mom.

When I spot the four-litre jar of cocktail olives stuffed with red pimento, I can't resist making a suggestion. "So — I'm just thinking out loud here — but what about going to the normal grocery store?"

"Didn't you see the olives I got?" asks Dad.

"It's hard to miss, Dad."

"Well, I got that jar for eight dollars. At the normal grocery store, who knows how expensive it would've been."

"How about a snack before dinner?" asks Mom.

"Yeah, I could nibble on something," Dad replies.

"Okay," says Mom. "Hmm, how about some olives?"

It's after eight and the summer sun is riding low on the horizon. The sky is a deep red. Even at this hour the late-July heat is convincing. I'm standing on the verandah drinking a beer with Dad. Three steaks are sizzling beside us on the grill. Mom found them in the bottom of the box freezer when she was putting away the groceries.

"We'll have these tonight," she said, holding them up on display. "I have some fresh veggies from the garden that'll go perfectly with them."

I've been given the task of barbecuing the meat.

"They're looking tasty," says Dad, peering over my shoulder. "I think they're probably ready."

"Well, I don't like them too bloody."

"Trust me, a good steak should be rare," says Dad matter-of-factly. "But I don't want to step on your toes, bud."

It's closer to nine when we sit to eat. The porch windows are open, and with the breeze I can finally feel an appreciable drop in the temperature. The sun is gone. I look down at my full plate of meat, potatoes, and garden vegetables. I take a deep breath and dig in.

"Pretty good," says Dad, holding a piece of pink steak up to the candle. "A little overdone maybe."

"I don't know about that," says Mom, meeting Dad's piece with her own. "I like it this way."

"Well, we do eat well," says Dad.

"We certainly do," agrees Mom. "We're just plain lucky."

We talk persistently throughout the meal, but of nothing significant. Mostly about the humidity, how much the grass has been growing, the animals, even about the vegetable garden and how it's flourishing in its new spot by the barn. The smell of Mom's peach crumble greets us on the porch before we're ready for it.

"Oh, listen, guys," says Mom. "I just realized the music has stopped. Could you run in and start it again, Iain? You'll probably have to shake the cord."

"Or try blowing on the inside," adds Dad.

I have to use both techniques simultaneously before I get it working.

"Bing sure is easy to listen to," says Mom, as his whistling picks up again.

When I return to the table, the candles are almost completely melted down. Mom's cutting the last of her meat into smaller pieces.

"Here," she says, "you guys can share this. It was so good, but I must admit I'm starting to feel a little full."

Dad receives his share on his plate nonchalantly. "Well," he says, "any ideas for tomorrow? Do we have any ribs in the freezer? I'm a sucker for ribs . . . well, ribs and bacon."

"I'm more of a sucker for soup," says Mom. "And cheeses. I love all different cheeses."

As my parents volley their culinary weaknesses back and forth like a shuttlecock, the music from the old CD player moves along freely and faithfully. "I almost forgot," says Mom. "I found another one of your notes sitting beside the bathroom sink this morning." There's a crumpled piece of paper sitting next to my plate that wasn't there before. "I almost threw it out by mistake."

For the past couple of weeks I've been jotting down notes on anything of significance I want to tell my pal Bob when I get back to Toronto. Because I usually just scribble these passing thoughts onto any old piece of scrap paper, Mom's been finding them all over the house. She dutifully returns them to me whenever they end up in her possession.

I wonder what my friends in Toronto are doing tonight. I haven't talked to them for a while. Actually, it's probably been more than a month. There's been no updating of any kind, no emails or phone calls. Even in this era of social networking, when it's so easy to stay connected, I've lost touch. Maybe it's for the best.

I watch my parents as they finish their meal, then look down at the scrawled note Mom's just returned to me. *Iain — do not forget about Marshall's big balls!* I fold the note three times and slip it meekly into my pocket.

Four

La Vie en Rose

I'M NOT SURE EXACTLY HOW THE TOPIC of the barn comes up. I certainly haven't mentioned it. It comes about errantly one night at supper, while I'm pondering Mom and Dad's differing methods of corn consumption. Dad, using the more traditional typewriter technique, eats one line along the cob before turning it, while Mom opts for the rotisserie method, eating while turning.

"You know," says Dad, "the barn hasn't been cleaned out for a long time."

I haven't shovelled manure in years. Not since high school. Growing up, I had transposed many barns' worth of packed animal feces, likely enough to fill an Olympic swimming pool or two. Digging out the sheep barn sometime in late August was an annual custom on the farm. Every couple of years this undesirable task would fall to my brother, Jimmy, and me. We would comply resentfully. The dimensions of the barn are large enough to amass a sizeable collection of sheep droppings but not quite big enough for a tractor or backhoe to enter, so the cleanout had to be done manually, with a couple of shovels, a pickaxe, and a wheelbarrow. We would dump each barrel-load onto the expanding pile behind the barn. Family and friends would then descend upon the nutrient-filled manure and fill bags and buckets with it to use as fertilizer. And then the cycle would begin again the next summer.

As we grew up and left home, the sheep barn was dug out less and less frequently. It's hot, demanding work, a chore best suited for two teenagers with energy to burn. And it's a job that, if pushed, you can put off for several years at a time. It just means that with each passing year the barn's floor rises in a slow, incessant tide of decaying shit.

"Are you sure?" questions Mom, wiping butter from her fingers with the edge of her napkin. "Didn't we hire the O'Bryant kids to do it a few times?"

"I don't think so."

"Well, that's ridiculous then; it should be done this year."

"Yeah, I'm sure the O'Bryant kids wouldn't mind coming up for a little extra pocket change," I add.

Dad drops his naked cob onto his plate. Mom glares at me. "All the O'Bryant kids are long gone. In fact, David just graduated with a degree in music and his band's doing quite well. I cut out an article in the paper about them to show you last week."

I can still remember babysitting the O'Bryants when I was twelve.

"We don't need the O'Bryants," reckons Dad. "We could do it. The three of us. It might be fun."

"It's great exercise too," says Mom.

"That's a great idea. But we don't even know if Iain's going to be around for much longer."

My weekly review had been a moderate success but it was rooted in summer, when listeners are looking for books to peruse at the cottage or on vacation. I'd just finished my last one the week prior. It ended as it had started, with little fanfare.

After my last review, one of the producers approached me as I was leaving the studio. She asked if I was going back to Toronto. I told her I wasn't really sure. Then she asked if I would be interested in covering for another producer who would be away. They would need me to start the first week of September. I would be a casual employee and would be offered other shifts as they arose.

I've never done any producing or real journalistic work before, and for a moment I thought about declining and heading back to Toronto. Considering my other options for employment either here or in Toronto — none — there was a certain degree of temptation. Then she told me my title would be associate producer, and that pretty much clinched it.

I did follow up with a few questions. Did associate producers receive benefits? "Not casual ones," she said. Not that I planned on it, but I was curious to know if associate producers had paid sick days. "Typically not," she answered, looking at her watch. I didn't know what else to ask so I said, "Okay, I'll try being an associate producer."

Armed with my new title, I decided half-heartedly to check apartment listings online. While a part of me had welcomed my summer-long retreat from urban gatherings, another part was skeptical about such extreme solitude. When you're in your late twenties, I don't think it's considered optimal for your best friend to be a nocturnal farm dog named Titan. In Toronto I would spend a few nights a week with friends. At the farm those friends had been replaced by animals. So if I started making more money, I thought it might make sense to leave the farm and move in with some people my own age.

I drove into the city to see a place, a modern basement apartment with stainless steel appliances but devoid of natural light. Turns out I'd be sharing it with a young professional couple, their mountain bikes, their caffeine-free energy drinks, and their penchant for reality TV. I stood in the doorway as they waited for a commercial break before showing me around the place. It was unnaturally ordered and tidy, and it smelled of citrus. "No smoking," they stressed several times. They were both allergic to second-hand smoke. "And we don't really drink or anything, either."

I thanked them and left. I shouldn't get ahead of myself anyway. Working spot-shifts would provide only a modest income, and all the apartments downtown were pricey — by my standards anyway — even the shared basements. And after that first and only visit to see an apartment, I decided socializing was overrated too.

Still, I haven't broached the topic of prolonging my stay on the farm with Mom and Dad. It will ultimately be up to them. As I pick corn from my teeth, I figure it's a good time to feel them out. "So I think I'll be here for a bit longer, around the farm, if that's okay with you guys. And I'm happy to help out with anything, you know, as my contribution."

"Of course," says Mom. "We really didn't expect you'd be leaving this soon anyway. Who'd ever want to leave Lilac Hill?"

Dad is peppering his second cob. "It's probably for the best, bud. That barn really needs a good cleanout."

In the next few days Dad's barn-refurbishing plan takes off. There is no possibility of avoidance or disruption. No delays or rain checks. The dig will start tomorrow.

After supper I go upstairs and lie down on the bed. I'm trying to recall more details about my past manure-digging experiences. I can remember the mini-assembly-line system my brother implemented to maximize our efficiency, and the way he was always able to use some form of circular logic or Socratic dialogue to dupe me into doing the worst parts of the job. I can remember the reversible basketball tank tops we wore as we worked, which we would inevitably remove a few hours into our shift and tie around our heads to keep the flies away. But I'm drawing a blank on all the stuff that concerns me now. Is it taxing work? Is there heavy lifting involved? How hot does the barn get? Do the sheep get in the way? Can Mom pick up a shovel? Does it smell? I think it has to smell.

I've been reminded of the health benefits for us, the labourers, by Mom and Dad, but more critically for the sheep. The sheep are going to love it.

I hear the familiar melody about twenty feet from the barn. There's no mistaking that powerful feminine voice. I lower my head and slow my pace. The only rule we've ever had for digging out the barn concerns the soundtrack. The first person in the barn gets to pick the music. That's it — that's the only rule. My brother and I had similar tastes in music, so regardless of who got there first, the chances were good we'd be digging to Digital Underground or The Band. From the sounds of it, Dad was first in the barn today. He's decided, enchantingly, that we'll be digging to French love songs. It's not that I don't love Edith Piaf. I do. She's great. I'm just not convinced she's best suited to keep me motivated while I dig out eight-year-old shit.

The temperature outside is uncomfortably hot; inside the barn it's stifling. The air greets me heavily, obnoxiously, like a foul hug. Flies are buzzing around Mom and Dad's heads in sparse clouds. They're both wearing white T-shirts (Mom's has a picture of a border collie, Dad's reads "Oxford University" across the front), knee-length shorts, and wide-brimmed safari hats. Mom and Dad have been productive. They've already removed about two square feet of manure from the north side of the barn.

"We left the pickaxe for you, bud," says Dad, holding it out for me like a souvenir. "Be careful; it's heavier than it looks."

He's right. I'd forgotten its impressive weight. The top layer of manure has been compressed by the herd into a hard crust. It needs to be broken up. It takes several blows with the pickaxe to loosen. When it's cracked and peeled back, a different smell, one equally pungent but much richer, earthier, is released. Now I remember. The smells in the barn are unsympathetically kaleidoscopic. Sweat is already running down my forehead and into my eyes. It stings.

Mom and Dad are unfazed. They work serenely. They haven't mentioned any of the things I'm focusing on: the heat or the smells or the flies or how the skin on the palms of my hands is starting to peel and blister. I should have worn gloves. They chat impulsively, cheerily as they dig. By noon the sheep have returned from pasture, gathering at the entrance. We've invaded their space but they haven't come as agitators, only observers. They watch us with crafty, inquiring eyes. They aren't hostile; instead they are calm, like granite.

For lunch we break outside the barn. Mom unwraps a peanut butter and banana sandwich and an apple for each of us. I eat the apple first and toss the core to the chickens. The sandwich tastes better than peanut butter and banana usually tastes, the way all food does after strenuous work.

It's easy to lose track of time in the barn. I've put off checking my watch for as long as I can and try desperately to underestimate how long it's been since the last check. I tell myself I've been digging for only forty minutes since the last time-check, secretly assured that it's been at least an hour. Then I look: thirty minutes. The disappointment burns worse than the sweat in my eyes. Dad, on the other hand, is checking his watch every five minutes.

After supper I'm tired and dehydrated. I lie on the couch, flipping aimlessly through the channels, drinking bottles of beer. I swiftly empty three and fall asleep with the baseball game on. It's late when I wake with a dry mouth and a headache. The TV has been turned off. I stumble to my room and topple face down on my bed. Within seconds I'm asleep.

The next morning, despite my hangover, I'm up early. I'm hoping to get a few hours of digging in before the heat becomes unbearable. Yesterday the worst hours were after lunch, when the afternoon sun made a sauna of the barn. I kept waiting for the sheep to walk in wearing flip-flops and with towels cinched around their waists. I must have spent close to eight hours in there, five during this undesirable period. Night digging is out of the question because the sheep are back inside by then. So morning — the earlier the better — is the time to dig.

I spend several valuable minutes searching for my work shorts. I have only one pair. I'd eagerly walked out of them yesterday as soon as I got back to the house, and left them on the laundry room floor. I'm standing in the laundry room now. They aren't here.

I detect some rustling upstairs. It must be Mom in the bathroom. I call up to her. "Hey, Mom, you haven't seen my work shorts, have you?"

"Uh, I don't think so."

"Well, they were on the floor last night and now they're gone."

"Which floor?'

"I don't know; I guess the laundry room."

"Oh, well then, they've been washed."

"What?"

"I must have washed them last night."

"So you have seen them?"

"Yeah, I guess so."

"Can I get into them?"

"No, I'm sure they're still soaked. Shouldn't take too long for them to dry today, though. It looks lovely out there. It still feels like the middle of summer."

I'm back upstairs now, burrowing peevishly in the back of my closet. I need to find something, anything. I don't have an extensive wardrobe to begin with, so my options are limited. I can't wear either of my two pairs of everyday shorts, because they will end up stained with sweat and manure. It's too hot for long pants of any kind. Even cotton sweatpants or ripped jeans would be unmanageably warm.

Dad's already outside getting started in the barn. How did he get up so early? Mom's proceeding from window to window, humming, closing them shut and pulling down the blinds. We open the windows before we go to bed to let the cool breeze flow through the house. But without air conditioning, the house, like the barn, heats up quickly during the day. It's already getting muggy in here. I can feel everything — the house, the land, my body — growing hotter by the minute. I can even feel my heart beating in my head. I wanted to be outside an hour ago. There must be something for me to wear.

"Have you checked your sister's closet?" calls Mom from her perch on the hall windowsill. She's still fussing with one of the blinds. "I think she left a box of her old clothes in there." Mom jumps down, saying she'll see me in the barn.

I haven't been in my sister's room, not once, since returning home. To keep the cats out the door is always left closed, and until now I've had no reason to go in. Nothing has changed. I move past her dusty awards collection from high school and her neatly arranged bookcase towards the closet. I open the closet door and see them sitting on top of a pile of old clothes: my sister's old Hawaiian shorts. They're baby blue and marked with white stylized flowery blossoms. There's a white drawstring in the front and two pockets painted on the bum. And the bastards are short — skanky short.

Back in my room I slip them on with regrettable ease. They're tight around my midriff. With only enough string to knot them once, they barely fit. I look at myself in the mirror. They leave very little to the imagination, providing an unfortunate view of my skinny white thighs and twig-like calves. My legs look like the legs of an old man who has spent weeks lying in a hospital bed — legs that have never felt the warm gaze of the sun, legs that have atrophied from neglect.

"Oh, great, you found a pair," declares Mom as I walk in the barn. "I knew you would."

Dad halts his work immediately and stands up straight. "Those look like girl's shorts, bud."

"I actually think the colour suits him. You don't usually see men wearing that shade of blue. It's unique."

I stare at my parents, from one to the other and back again, for what feels like an hour. They're smiling devotedly. I say nothing. My face is expressionless. I retrieve my pickaxe and begin to work.

"It's fascinating," says Dad. He's speaking more slowly now, and pauses vexingly between each word. "Your legs really are *quite* skinny, aren't they?"

I'm not sure whether the question is rhetorical or he's hoping for a reply. I continue moving the dried muck around with my pickaxe. Mom answers for me.

"Yes, he sure does," she says. "Skinny little ankles too." She's leaning on her spade now. Dad's elbow is supported by the shaft of his shovel, his opposite hand resting on his hip. "Don't you remember what the nurses said when he was born?"

"No, I can't remember."

I've decided that breaking up the manure crust is the worst job. But in this insipid trio, it will always be my job. I raise the pickaxe over my head and slam it down into the firm mat. The music is louder today and echoes off the barn walls. Mom and Dad have adapted by yelling back and forth at one another. Edith Piaf has been given the day off. Today we are digging to the collected works of Gilbert and Sullivan.

"Well, they said he was all legs, and then everyone started calling him 'Chicken Legs' — even the nurses."

"Yeah, I can see that," adds Dad, examining my exposed legs. "That's fair; they're quite chickeny."

On my way back from dumping my sixth or seventh full wheelbarrow, I stop several feet from the barn door. I can hear Mom and Dad.

"I was just thinking," Dad's saying. "Iain's legs are almost more like the sheep than the chickens, because proportionally the sheep legs are probably even skinnier than the chickens'."

"You know, I think you're right. They're a touch closer to sheep legs than chicken legs."

I enter the barn and grab my pickaxe. Mom and Dad are looking from the sheep to my legs and back to the sheep again. I slam the point down hard into the manure. They are nodding in amazed agreement, as if they've just excavated the Ark of the Covenant. On my next swing I want to miss the muck altogether and bury the sharp point directly in my shin. My skinny white shin.

On morning three I'm sore. I'm stiff. I've given up trying to get a head start and have slept in — fuck it! Blisters have formed on my hands in bunches. From the bathroom window I see Mom and Dad. They're laughing. Probably at something one of the sheep did. Or maybe an old story Mom just recounted. I'm feeling angry. What's their problem? I don't want them to be so cheerful. I want them to plod along silently, slowly, petulantly, because that's what I would be doing if I had rolled out of bed earlier. And that's what I will be doing when I get there. Now I'm just standing at the window frowning, swearing, bitter, and sore.

I don't know what the temperature is but it's the muggiest day yet. It has to be the muggiest day of the year. By the time I get to the barn, my forehead is glazed with perspiration like a doughnut. I am, however, growing used to the smells. It's taken until day three, but the manure actually smells normal. I'm thankful for that at least.

"You're moving a little gingerly today, bud. Are you feeling all right?" asks Dad.

"I'm fine." I pile another shovelful of manure into the wheelbarrow. "I guess maybe a little stiff. I have no idea why the backs of my legs would be stiff."

"A little strange," says Dad.

"You're just not used to using them, I guess," says Mom, as she heads out of the barn with a full barrow.

By the middle of the afternoon we're close. In another hour or two the barn will be new again. The mound out back has grown like a smelly cyst on the land. It doesn't seem possible that we could have removed all that mess from our snug barn. I'm not even concerned about my blisters anymore — the blisters that have popped, exposing the raw skin underneath; the blisters neither of my parents got. My feelings of hostility have faded with the possibility of a fourth day of digging.

As Dad wheels the last barrow of muck out to the hill, Mom and I stand in the barn, admiring its vacuity.

"We did it. Doesn't it look great?"

"It does," I agree. My shirt is wet from sweat. We are all sweating, but no one as much as me.

I've showered and changed. I'm dozing on the verandah when the distinct pop of a champagne cork perks me up. Dad walks out carrying the bottle, wrapped in a tea towel, in one hand and three glasses by their bases in the other. Mom follows with a tray. They've insisted we celebrate.

"Well, this is a treat," Mom's saying.

"A well-deserved treat," answers Dad. "I know it's a little exuberant, but we deserve it."

Their faces are still flushed from the work and the heat, but not heavy with fatigue like my own. I'm parched, and the sight of the bottle delights me. Dad pours us each a glass of the bubbly golden liquid, and we toast the hollow barn.

"I bet this was harder than the work you'll have to do at your new job," says Dad.

"Yes, this should be a congrats for the new job too," adds Mom.

I nod.

"What is your new job again?"

"Associate producer," I say.

"Pretty exciting," says Mom.

"Indeed," agrees Dad.

"And maybe even if you're an associate producer," suggests Mom, "you'll still be around next summer, and we can dig again."

"We can start making it a tradition," says Dad.

I can hear the blue jays and swallows in the trees to my left. Their presence causes both cats lying beside me to stir.

To accompany the drink, Mom has assembled some goodies: cheese, crackers, grapes, mixed nuts, salami, olives. Every so often she waves her hand overtop of the plate to keep the flies from landing. The flies are more interested in the snacks than I am. After another glass or two my appetite should emerge. Dad's nibbling on a handful of nuts, but mainly we focus on the cold champagne.

I'm picking at one of the blisters on my hand with a fingernail when Dad clears his throat, confirming that he's been constructing a thought. "Now, without getting into a lecture here," he says, topping up our glasses, "in his poem 'The Prelude,' Wordsworth talks about what he calls spots of time. These are moments for everybody when they can get a sense of things, actually see into the life of things." Dad fills his own glass last. He rests the empty bottle carefully beside his seat and grabs another handful of nuts. "Look out there," he says, motioning to the rolling fields in front of us. "I think I know what he means."

We sit contemplatively. Even at dusk the air hasn't cooled. Summer is packing up to go but hasn't left just yet. We sip our champagne willingly; I drain half my glass in one mighty pull. Every so often a car passes on the road. In front of us on the grass, both dogs are asleep.

The digging is done. My shovel and pickaxe will be replaced by a keyboard, monitor, and phone. I'm going to be doing some serious journalistic work; I'm going to be an associate producer. As far as I know, associate producers don't dig sheep manure. They produce quality radio. And they earn a salary and contribute to society. And they start a pension. They are adults. And because they're adults, they can't spend full days at a farm with their parents. They have their own apartments, with their own furniture.

I balance my chair back on its rear legs, stretching my feet out in front of me. I look over at the slumbering dogs, then towards the pond, the fields, and out to the wandering sheep. Some nibble the grass; others stand chewing their cud, watching us complacently. They appear perfectly oblivious of their subtle yet necessary role in our little celebration.

Fall

Five

Handy Man

ONE OF SEPTEMBER'S ANNUAL PROMISES — to lessen the heat of summer and marshal in the crisper, milder conditions of fall — has been broken. There's been no breach in the August swelter, and each humid degree this September has felt like two.

While the heat has endured, our routine at the farm has swerved off its summer course. Dad's lessened his professorial workload in recent years, but he still lectures at the university a couple of days a week, holds office hours, and continues doing his own research. Mom also seems to be engaged in a variety of commitments away from the farm, everything from community meetings to yoga. We've been seeing less of one another, coming and going at different times of day.

I've started my new job downtown. My alarm wakes me just after 7 a.m. I shower, dress, and am out the door by 7:45 a.m. to sit in traffic and creep along the highway. The commute is around an hour or so, and I'm expected at work by 9 a.m. sharp for the daily story meeting. Every morning I have to come up with two viable story ideas to pitch to the rest of the team. I've been arriving with just enough time to grab a cup of coffee and fret some more about the dubious ideas I'm about to pitch.

Once everyone has offered their two ideas, the weaker ones are cast aside. The senior producer assigns two or three stories to each associate producer to "chase" for that afternoon's show. I didn't know what chasing was for my entire first week. Essentially it involves finding suitable guests for a story, tracking them down, conducting a pre-interview over the phone, and writing the script for the on-air interview.

On my first day I was shown to my desk. It was my first-ever office desk. I wondered what pictures I should bring in to personalize my space the way everyone else had done. The desk was mine for about nine minutes, until I was shuffled off to the temp desk. I was told as I stood beside the desk, papers hugged to my chest, not to get too comfortable, because it's always hard to predict where the temp seat will be from week to week.

I find that I'm not nearly efficient enough to take a lunch break, and have been eating at my desk while plodding ahead. Sometime around 6 p.m. I'm usually tossing my knapsack into the back seat of my car, drained, preparing myself for another hour of horns and exhaust while I inch my way back to the farm. After supper I sit with the cats, scouring the newspaper and the Internet for ideas for the next morning until my eyes start to slip shut.

The farm hasn't been much of a refuge from work. There's a lot to do to prepare for winter. After we shovelled out the sheep barn there was still the chicken coop to tidy, the wood stove to sweep, some painting to do, and gardens to turn over. My first two weeks of September have been the most hectic since my return home.

Thankfully they've scheduled someone else to work on Friday this week, so I've been conscripted to help Mom with her baking. I suppose it's a reasonable request. With each pass through the kitchen, I consume my share. She tells me she's planning to bake some chocolate chip cookies, a lemon loaf or two, and maybe some apple walnut bread if we have time. I actually don't mind baking. There are worse ways to spend a couple of hours than sifting a few cups of flour and melting sticks of unsalted butter in a pan. "Happy to help," I say.

"The first thing you can do is collect the eggs for me," Mom says, chin tucked down while tying her apron behind her neck. "I need a few and we may as well use today's."

"Oh," I say. I was doing that chore a lot when I first returned, collecting the eggs. At first I volunteered to do it instead of, say, taking out the trash. Now I know better. Between the animals eating our peelings and table scraps, the compost pile out back, and my parents' prudent ways, there's very little garbage to speak of. So strolling down to the end of the lane handling a single plastic bag of scentless paper trash is my new favourite chore. Collecting the eggs has gone the other way.

You might assume it's a breezy task, an enjoyable one. I did. But our chicken coop is a dark, eerie place. The white paint is starting to peel off the outside walls, and the door sags from its rusty hinges. Inside the smells are sharp.

Young and old chicken droppings acknowledge you with each step. There are noises too; strange chirps and clucks and scratches come at you from all corners. The ceiling is adorned with cobwebs, and if you enter too quickly you might even see a mouse scurry off into one of its tunnels in the floor. Did I mention it smells? We've just cleaned it out and laid down fresh bags of wood chips, but the hens' ability to soil the floor in such little time is striking. It's disconcerting to think that this is where all of Mom's baking begins.

My main issue with the coop isn't simply its crappy ambience but also its eccentric inhabitants. Chickens aren't timid like many of the farm animals here. The moment you step through the creaky door, the feckless creatures descend upon you like zombies, moving mechanically, wings stretching, jerking their heads up, down, pecking the floor. And like zombies, they are categorically obsessed with eating. They circle you in a stunned mob, assuming you've brought grain, grass, peelings, or anything they can feed on. There's no question that they would greedily peck away at my brain if given the chance. It's not that I hate chickens — it's hard to hate something that has the mental capacity of an earthworm — I just don't trust their erratic behaviour and clan mentality.

In the shed I step into my black rubber boots and grab one of the straw-lined baskets. I thought I'd been asked to help with the baking in the kitchen? This isn't baking. I'm not in the kitchen. This is much worse. This is collecting.

That's another thing: the term itself is irritating. *Grappling* would be a more accurate word to describe the task than *collecting*. The hens battle instinctively, spiritedly, as any mother would while defending her infant. I now refuse to set foot in the coop without my armour — a pair of winter work gloves I found in the shed. The chicken's peck is tenacious, but not forceful enough to penetrate the thickly lined leather gloves. Carelessly reaching into one of their occupied nesting boxes with a bare hand is lunacy, no matter how golden and delicious those yolks are. Their unblunted beaks will pierce human skin as easily as wet paper towel.

I unhitch the latch loudly and knock on the chicken coop door. That's my warning for the mice to scurry away, since I'm not keen on seeing them. I pull the door open and clear my throat.

"Morning, ladies," I say, taking a jittery step inside.

All of the hens but two have already departed their nesting boxes. Covering my nose with one hand, I nab five eggs from the first three nests. Then I move on to the remaining two. The last box is employed by one of the largest birds, a fat auburn hen with a formidable beak. I recognize her instantly from previous run-ins. She's bold and stubborn and sits atop her eggs like Jabba the Hutt. I start by lulling her into a false state of confidence.

"Hey, girl, don't mind me . . . just here to check on your feed . . . an innocent feed check is all . . . you gotta keep your strength up with all that sitting around you do." I slowly move towards the feeder. "Yup, looks like you guys are good to go." That's when I swivel and strike her nest in one quick motion.

Her resistance is equally fleet. She lands a counterstrike directly on my exposed wrist. It isn't a kill shot by any means; she doesn't draw blood. Yet her calm demeanour, and the speed and precision with which the blow is delivered, is enraging.

I wait. I try again. Same result. I turn to the observant group. "What's everybody looking at? Everybody just shut up."

I bend down now, taking my time while moving closer to her. I watch her ruffle up her breast feathers. "Now listen, I'm not going to hurt you. I just want that egg. Just chill. I'm going to move slowly." I hold up my empty free hand as evidence that I've come in peace. I start inching it towards her underside. She's still. "That's it, that's it . . . See, we're friends." And just as the tips of my fingers touch the straw she lands her third blow, forcing me to stumble backwards.

"Fucking bitchy shit hen!" I scream. My voice is strained with emotion, and before I know it I've punched Jabba right in her chicken face. Well, more in the plumage between her neck and face. It's not a jab but a perfectly executed right hook. If she'd been wearing a mouthguard it would have shot out of her mouth along with a spray of hen saliva. The chicken is more surprised than hurt. She jumps from her nesting box, retreating to the far end of the coop. I remove the last egg with a shaky hand and place it in my basket with the others.

I turn to leave but pause at the door, saying over my shoulder to the suddenly quiet coop, "Right, from now on you hens just have to be cool, okay? That's not how I wanted it to go down. No, not like that. Everybody just needs to be cool . . . just be cool." One of the newer pullets lets out a mellow cluck. Most of them ignore me and continue pecking at the metal feeder.

Back inside I find Mom using a wooden spoon to fold the wet ingredients into the dry.

"Don't you need the eggs first, before mixing all of that?" I ask.

"Yup, everybody's already in the pool," she says, licking some batter off her baby finger.

"What do you mean? I have the eggs right here." I raise the basket up beside my face.

"Oh, shoot. I ended up using yesterday's from the fridge." I lower the basket and my head in unison. "Well, don't worry; maybe we'll have an omelette for lunch or a toasted western. I know how much you like those."

"I guess I'm done then, right?"

"Done? No, no," says Mom. "You see those lemons over there? It's time to zest!"

I'm back in the kitchen post-baking, looking to top up my coffee and sample our yield, when Mom pops up from under the sink, a tea towel slung around her shoulders like a neck brace. "It's bad news under there," she says. "There's a leak. You better take a look."

I sigh. I sigh because it's the start of the weekend, I've been helping her in the kitchen for most of the morning, and now I want to drink my coffee alone. And I sigh because I've been noticing an unsettling trend. Mom and Dad seem to think I'm handy. I'm not sure exactly why or when this assumption began; it couldn't be based on my barren record of fixing things.

I bend down on one knee and look at the pipe

descending from the bottom of the sink like a metal root. I wish I could just sift some flour or measure out a couple of cups of demerara sugar.

"Well, it seems fine to me, Mom. Nothing to worry about down here," I say.

"Well, shouldn't we try turning the tap back on? Before we jump to any conclusions?"

Again I sigh, louder this time. "I suppose."

I hear Mom twist the tap and almost instantly a steady stream of water starts trickling through a hole in the pipe.

I wouldn't exactly pigeonhole Mom as a plumbing virtuoso; I completely understand her wish for help. But I too am no plumber. There's a problem with the sink, fair enough. But it's me helplessly shining a flashlight onto the torrent of water, not Dad, so I'm not ready to admit it. Dad's at the university yesterday and today, marking essays.

"You know, it doesn't look too bad, Mom. Are you sure this isn't normal?" The water's pouring out faster now and is beginning to pool on the plywood below. "How often do you look down here anyway? I think I remember reading something about a bit of spillover being the norm."

She whips me with the towel. "That's a leak. Something isn't working right down there. I don't know much about sinks, but it looks to me like the catch basin has cracked. You know, the thing the strainer sits in."

I pause. "Well, yeah, I know it's the catch basin . . . sort of obvious . . . I'm just curious if you think it needs to be dealt with . . . today-ish."

"Of course it does," she replies. "Just pop up to the hardware store; someone there will show you what to get."

After wrestling the old, broken catch basin out of the sink with two different sets of pliers, a wrench, a rubber mallet, and Mom encouraging me like a ringside manager, I'm off to the store.

I pull up in my baby blue Toyota, the licence plate held together by hockey tape, alongside a row of gleaming pickup trucks. I roam aimlessly up and down the rows of tools and lumber for twenty minutes before I finally spot Rich. Rich sports a shabby red vest, two or three sizes too small. The front is forced open by his large pail of a belly. I stroll up to him, tossing the cracked catch basin up in the air and catching it.

"I'll be needin' a new one of these bad boys," I announce. "They don't make 'em like they used to."

Rich, hunch-shouldered and stubble-faced, remains focused on restocking the wall of small washers in front of him. He directs me to the aisle of plumbing parts with a casual wave of his hand, revealing a patch of wetness in his armpit. "That's just a small part," he says over his shoulder. "Won't take you two minutes to put her in."

Any allusion of shop-teacher charm that Rich inadvertently exuded in person has vanished over the phone. I've been back home for an hour and am forced to once again seek help from him. But he wants no part of my problem.

"Listen, I'm not sure what else to tell you; it should just fit in easy. There's nothing to it."

"Well, it's weird, all right," I say. "It just doesn't fit."

"I don't know what else to tell you. You sure you bought the right piece?" Rich is gruff and hurried.

I'm standing over the sink cradling the phone between my shoulder and ear. The new catch basin is sitting an inch higher than it should. It's meant to be flush with the bottom of the sink — that much I know. "Oh, wait, do I have to hammer it into place or something? I have a mallet available." I pick up the mallet in my right hand and raise my arm, poised to strike.

"What? No! No hammering or malleting. It should just fit."

"Well, maybe I'll just try it a different way." Saying these words, I hear their foolishness. Trying it a different way is impossible. We're dealing with one part and one hole in the bottom of the sink. There is only one way for the part to fit.

"I really can't believe it," I say to Mom. "Rich is a bitch. He sold me a defective part. It just comes down to bad luck, I guess. So, what do you feel like for lunch? Some nice scrambled eggs would be —"

"It doesn't look defective," she says, picking the shimmering piece of hardware out of the sink and eyeing it closely. "It looks like a quality piece to me."

"Fine, give me the damn thing," I say, grabbing it back. This is ridiculous. I'm a grown man. I can grow a beard. I have a framed diploma. I just have to think it through logically. Every problem has a solution. I take a deep breath and focus.

Ten minutes later I'm back on the phone, this time with our neighbour Earl.

"Hi, Earl, it's Iain from up the road." We exchange a few pleasantries before getting to the meat of the call. "So, Mom's having a bit of a problem with the catch basin in the kitchen sink. I'm thinking it's defective." I've never known Earl to decline a call for help. He can fix anything.

"Would you like me to come down and take a look?"

"That would be great," I say.

Mom and I sit in silence while we wait for Earl. "I'll put on some music," she says, trying to lighten my mounting anxiety. I hear her shuffling through the CDs. "Oh, I love this song," Mom says. She's put on The Proclaimers' "500 Miles." She's already humming the tune before it starts. I'm slouched over the table, hoping Earl will arrive soon and confirm that the part is defective.

Three long Proclaimers songs later, Earl appears at the front door in a red plaid shirt. He smiles and waves. I let him in. After looking at the new catch basin for less than three seconds, Earl asks if I took it apart before putting it in.

"One part goes in the sink and the other screws in from underneath. That's what holds it in place," he says.

I stand beside Earl, looking down at the hole in the sink. He's so obviously right.

"It's not a big deal," he says. "Just a good thing you didn't do anything stupid, like hammer it in or something. You'd be surprised what some people will try."

It takes Earl less than five minutes to install the new attachment. Afterwards he chats with Mom about the usual things: the weather, this year's crops, the animals. He wonders if we've seen any rats around the chicken coop this summer. I finally top up my mug with the now burnt coffee and head for the couch.

My embarrassing debacle with the sink hardware isn't a huge surprise. It's not that I'm a complete failure when it comes to household chores, but I'm also a far cry from Mike Holmes. I fall somewhere in between Holmes and Failure Guy, probably just off-centre in the direction of failure. And I've always been this way. Like my crooked teeth, it's probably genetic — an inherited flaw. To be honest, I've never really had much of an interest in repairing or constructing or even tinkering.

Instead, like Mom and my sister, Jean, I enjoy cooking. I make a passable tomato sauce from scratch and decent home made soups, not to mention my peanut butter cookies. I appreciate the culinary arts. And cleaning's another thing. Give me the choice between a chainsaw and a vacuum cleaner and I'll happily reach for the Hoover. I can breeze through the carpets of an entire house in under an hour without leaving a single footprint. I'm not even fazed by an old-fashioned broom and dustpan. I enjoy sweeping. I find it strangely gratifying. If you think about it, I would have been quite a catch in the fifties. Not as a virile husband, of course, but as an apple-cheeked housewife. It's amazing. And by amazing, I mean dejecting.

I remember the summer I worked for the university grounds crew. I was well into my third month of employment when Doug, the brusque backhoe operator, finally muttered his first and only words to me. I'd been working closely with Doug every day. He'd been at his job for more than thirty years and had seen many students come and go each summer. He must have been in his early sixties. He was strong but wiry, and had white hair and a hoary stubble beard. I never had any problems with him. I liked him. He was a man of few words — so what?

I was wielding an old wooden-handled spade, digging a ten-foot-long trench to plant some shrubs. Doug, on his smoke break, was watching from his tractor, sitting back in his seat resting a foot on the wheel. As I paused to wipe the sweat from my face, Doug stood, and with his burning smoke still dangling off his lip, walked up to me and put his hand on my shoulder with a mighty grip. Was he finally going to commend my work? Or maybe insist that I'd put in my time for the day and he would graciously take over? It was a scorching day, after all, and I'd been going at the trench for almost an hour. I was starting to feel a trifle flushed.

"Well," he said thoughtfully, "I hope for the girls' sake you can fuck better than you swing a shovel." And with that he released a scratchy cackle, spat on the ground, and hobbled back to his tractor.

On Sunday night my parents again put me to the test. I hear them calling from upstairs. They're watching TV with a bowl of popcorn between them, each with a paper towel resting on their lap.

"We're thinking of going to bed soon, but there's a mystery on PBS we'd like to see," says Dad. "Do you remember how to set the VCR to tape?"

Obviously I haven't set anything to record on VHS since the mid-nineties. "Do we still have a VCR?" I ask.

"Course," Dad replies. "We need something to watch all our videos."

I can't recall the last time either of my parents has

watched a VHS video. I quickly scan the bookcase by the wall, which displays their collection. I can make out only three. *Animals Are Beautiful People: The Secret Lives of Wildlife* is in a white box with a cartoon giraffe smiling broadly on the front. Next to it is *The 1992 Major League Baseball Season in Review*; its box is in much worse condition, faded and torn at the corners. Third is a black cassette without a box. A handwritten label on the front clearly reads HONEY I SHRUNK THE KIDS WITHOUT COMMERCIALS!!! Dad's right; thank God we still have a VCR.

"You know, Dad, a lot of people just record TV right onto their satellite box these days. It's called PVR, and they can watch it anytime they want just by pushing a button. No tapes or cords needed."

"I don't know about that," Dad says suspiciously. "Besides, we still have all those blank tapes to use."

"Waste not, want not," Mom adds, picking a kernel off her paper towel and popping it into her mouth.

I nod and move to my least favourite area of the room, the back of the TV. It's a lifeless jungle, a mess of tangled cords, power bars, and dust. There isn't much space, and with the lights dimmed it's difficult to see. The room is stuffy and I can sense my forehead starting to glisten. Meanwhile my parents are enjoying the commercials, laughing out loud at the animated gecko with a British accent. He's trying to sell car insurance and is doing a fine job.

"Sorry to interrupt, Dad, but I'm not really sure which cords to change here."

"Oh, I don't think you need to change the cords. I think there's a button on the front of the machine or something."

I swivel around and sink down in front of the TV on my stomach. The next ad is for a new low-calorie sports drink being promoted by hockey star Sidney Crosby.

"Huh, remind me to look into that," Dad says to no one in particular.

Mom perks up, licking the tips of her salty fingers. "What, you mean that sports drink?"

"Yeah," says Dad. "It has zero calories. I could use that."

"But you're not a professional athlete. You don't need that."

"But I work out. And I lose more than water when I sweat."

As my parents debate Dad's hydrating needs, I'm becoming increasingly confused by the VCR. I can't find a Record button anywhere.

"So why don't you shake some salt on your hand and lick it off after a workout? That's what my dad used to do."

"No, no, they say you should never do that. And anyway, I need more than salt. Potassium, for example."

"So eat a banana."

"Um, sorry, guys," I say. "Are you definitely sure this thing records?"

After a moment's pause my parents are up out of their seats and joining me on the floor. Dad pushes his glasses atop his head and squints at the front panel. Mom kneels beside him. She's brought a pillow from the couch with her for her knees. Her hand is resting on Dad's back.

"What do we have here?" he asks.

In the snug, stuffy space in front of the TV, three's definitely a crowd. I won't be much help, so I leave my parents on the floor.

The air in my bedroom is anchored and thick. It's difficult to sleep. I'm brooding over what stories I'm going to pitch at tomorrow's meeting. I have no ideas. None. Maybe something about plumbing, how complex it has become in the twenty-first century.

Lying on my back watching the ceiling fan swirl around and around, I eventually hear Mom's excited congratulations to Dad as he successfully sets the VCR.

Six

No Rest for the Unweary

THIS MORNING AFTER MY PORRIDGE I sit in my room to "write." Staring at the white computer screen, I use my left index finger to pull down and then snap my bottom lip against my top lip. It makes a funny sound. Well, not funny per se, but there is a sound. It proves entertaining for much longer than anticipated. My lip tires of the game before I do.

I've worked only two shifts this week. Two days of being an associate producer. What does that make me for the other five days? And those two days weren't exactly reassuring. I strolled into the story meeting a few minutes early, feeling unusually confident. I felt I had two strong ideas to pitch. Everyone seemed energized after the weekend, and the meeting was going well. Pens skated along notepads, people were laughing and nodding and passing articles from the paper along with mini-doughnuts someone had brought in.

And then it was my turn. I had the attention of the group, an abruptly quiet, suspicious group. All eyes turned on me. But as I started to explain my ideas, those same eyes moved on, finding other things to explore — the white ceiling tiles or tiny pieces of lint on the floor. Laughs were replaced by yawns. Pens lay frozen to the table.

"Okay, well, another idea I've been thinking about," I say, flipping through my papers, "is a little different. I'm thinking we could do a story about walking."

"Walking? How so?"

"Well, I'm not exactly sure. I just think walking is a good thing for people to do and it's underrated."

"You mean just walking, like strolling outside?'

"Sure, just walking."

"Sorry, Iain," another associate producer said, tossing her pad onto the table, "what exactly do you think the story is?"

"Well, that's a valid question. Couldn't we maybe talk to people who like to run or something, and compare them to people who like to walk? It just seems to me, with all the popularity of running, walking doesn't get the credit it deserves. I always see people out running. Everybody thinks that to be healthy you have to run."

The room was silent.

"Okay, thanks for the idea, Iain. I think that's it for this morning, guys. Let's get to work."

Five minutes later the senior producer assigned me a story about deer whistles.

I spend part of my next few hours pacing around the room, reading aloud in a Cockney accent from a paperback copy of *A Concise History of the Theatre* with pages 113 to 176 missing. I find it under my bed when I'm bouncing a rubber ball off the wall trying to see how many times I can catch it without a drop. When I start screaming some pretty heinous insults at myself after fumbling the ball on throw 143 (six away from a new personal best), I figure a change of scene might help.

I shamble into the kitchen in my slippers and slap together a pathetic-looking peanut butter and honey sandwich. Aside from Meg, the old border collie, who's watching me intensely, I eat it alone, not realizing that I'm collecting drops of honey on my shirt. It's been escaping out the back of the sandwich with each bite. I'm licking the honey off my shirt when Mom walks into the kitchen carrying a basket of clean laundry.

"Are you eating honey off your shirt again?" she asks indifferently.

"What?" I say. "No! Well, yes, but what do you mean 'again'?"

"I saw you doing that last week too. What's wrong? Are you overly tired?"

"No, I'm fine."

"That honey on your shirt says you're tired. It's a calling card of fatigue. Plus I can see it in your eyes. I hope you don't have to work any more shifts this week."

"I'm feeling fine, Mom, but, you know, when people are actually tired, the last thing they want to hear is that they look tired."

"Okay. But you don't care now, because you're not tired."

"But you thought I was."

"I still think you are."

"What?"

"I just think you should go to bed earlier tonight, that's all." She's picking socks out of the basket now and balling them together.

"Mom, I went to bed at nine thirty last night, like, an hour before you and Dad."

"You need your sleep, though, Iain. It's very important."

The truth is, I am tired — I'm exhausted. Those dark circles under my eyes are genuine. I've been going through these dry spells lately when sleep becomes inexplicably scarce. One night I'll sleep through until morning uninterrupted; then the next three or four nights will be spent lying on my side, the covers balled up beside me, while I stare vacantly at the wall. I just lie there frustrated, struggling to restrain my spinning thoughts, thinking and thinking about thinking, for hours.

It likely has something to do with sitting around the farm most days at my desk, bent over my laptop, tapping my keyboard intermittently. Or maybe it's because for the past several months I've been calling goodnight to my parents with the same childish inflection I had as a boy, before scurrying off to the same bed and crawling between the same blue sheets with yellow crescent moons I first used when I was eight. It's probably a little of both.

These restless nights leave me agitated, lethargic, melancholic. More so than a mind, a good night's sleep is a terrible thing to waste. And that's what's most troubling: I'm trading away sleep in an unfair deal. I'm not getting drunk from expensive whisky and waking up in a stranger's bed naked, with a lampshade on my head. No, I'm isolated in the countryside, sitting by the fire with Mom and Dad, finishing up the weekend crossword puzzle by trying to think of a three-letter word for *sarcastic*. That's a tepid mug of chamomile tea I'm sipping, not tequila. It's rarely that I'm not tucked into bed with a book by 10 p.m. Yet still, sleep ignores me.

This morning, before I had my porridge, I woke from a particularly frustrating night. I dozed sporadically for maybe three hours, even though I spent nine curled up in bed. I watched the lenient October sun appear between my blinds sometime around six and slowly grow brighter until two thin shafts of yellow light were spotlighting the base of my bed. In the bathroom, splashing cold water on my face, I found a sticky note with *wry!* written in my mother's hand stuck to the vanity mirror.

You already know where my day went from there. The honey has caked onto my shirt now. I'm helping Mom fold a massive king-sized sheet for her bed. We do this without talking, and I'm thankful for the quiet. It doesn't last long. Dad comes in from feeding the sheep and collecting the eggs.

"You're looking tired, bud," he says. "Are you sleeping enough these days?"

"Yes, I'm fine."

"How many hours are you getting?" he wonders as he sits to unlace his boots.

"I'm not sure. Definitely more than four."

"Four? That's not nearly enough. You need at least eight to ten. You should try going to bed earlier tonight."

"Much earlier," echoes Mom.

"It's not really about *when* I go to bed; it's that I'm not really sleeping *while* in bed."

"That's probably because you're too tired to sleep," says Mom.

"Definitely," agrees Dad. "And some people need more sleep than others. Sounds like you're one of them. What's that on your shirt?" He's moved over to the sink, where he's washing the eggs and handing them to Mom to dry.

"He spilled honey on himself again," answers Mom, shaking her head disapprovingly.

Dad holds up one of the wet brown eggs he's just collected from the coop. "Well, I suppose honey on his shirt is better than egg on his face."

Mom tries to hold her serious face but bursts into a giggling fit, doubling over into Dad's side like a domino. She bumps him just enough that he has to take a step back to keep his balance. The two are still laughing as I head upstairs.

Mom and Dad are asleep. I've popped some corn and am lying in front of the TV. At the farm, television is still a novelty to me. We never had cable when I was growing up, and I didn't own a TV in Toronto and rarely had the opportunity to watch one. It's late, and although tired I'm still hoping to squeeze in another hour or two of the moving pictures.

After instinctively scanning through all the channels three or four times, I'm forced to choose between an infomercial trying to sell me a vibrating abdominal belt and a horror movie called *The Mothman Prophecies*. Considering that my popcorn was gone in five minutes and I've moved on to a bowl of cheese curds, I stay on the infomercial for only a few minutes. I'd love to actually meet these actors. Get inside their heads. Find out what motivates them. Do these infomercial spots figure into their childhood dreams and aspirations? Or are they aware of their inherent ridiculousness?

I flip the channel over to *The Mothman Prophecies*. I remember hearing about this film a few years ago — it's adapted from a novel of the same name and generated substantial buzz. I scan the information on the satellite guide. The movie is set in a small West Virginia town where a reporter from Washington, D.C., investigates several strange encounters, unusual sightings, and mysterious phone calls. It's believed that a large supernatural moth-like creature is responsible for the chaos. I haven't seen a good horror movie in a while.

My introduction to horror films started early, when I was a wide-eyed seven-year-old. I remember sneaking out of bed and furtively crawling down the carpeted hall on my forearms and knees like a Navy Seal. Using the screams as my compass, I would converge on my older brother and a group of his teenage pals, slung over the couches in our TV room. It was the golden era of the horror genre. Fans had the luxury of choosing from a wide range of villains, the likes of which had never been seen before. There was the dream-invading Freddy Krueger, the machete-wielding Jason Voorhees, the demented Michael Myers, and even that homicidal doll from *Child's Play*.

Chucky, as he's known, quickly became my favourite for two reasons. One, because of his surprisingly sharp wit coupled with his peerless comedic timing, and two, because I figured that if ever faced with any of these hellions, I would have my best chance against the rubber doll with tiny hands.

The slasher films of the late 1970s and 1980s were built on clichés and relied almost exclusively on bloody violence and excessive gore. For me, peering through the tiny opening between the wall and the door in my jammy-jams, these predictable plotlines and extravagant death scenes were both alluring and terrifying, a most unfortunate coupling for a vulnerable seven-year-old.

The images of these killers hiding in my closet or crouching behind the shower curtain consumed me in the way most children of that age obsess over boy bands or professional athletes. Unable to sleep, I would be forced to confess the details of my illicit late-night viewings to Mom. Her disappointment soon led to anger. But Mom's not one to carry her temper long, and inevitably she would set it aside. Her anger would evolve into support, insisting that those awful characters were completely fictional and imaginary. We would sit together over a cup of warm milk or a bowl of her homemade soup as she explained in great detail how some Hollywood film screenwriter had been paid to invent the scariest creature he could imagine and then write a story about it. Like any business, the point was to make as much money as possible, so the scarier the better. She would always accentuate the fact that these monsters were conceived in someone's head and born on the set of a movie, never borrowed from real life. "It's not reality," she would remind me over and over again, dunking a chunk of cookie into her mug of milk. "It's just pretend."

On the occasions when her consoling words weren't enough, Dad would be summoned and asked to declaw any potential threat that might be looming in my closet, under my bed, or, most often, in my head. When words and ideology weren't enough, the sheer physical presence of Dad clad in boxer shorts and a tattered undershirt always carried the trump card of reassurance.

But as the years passed, my nightmares lingered. My mental maturity had ignored its assigned task. Instead of leading me away from these fabricated scenarios of night-time killers, my supposedly wiser mind paved a straighter road to the elaborate plotlines and frightening characters. I wondered why my older brother, the source of all the slasher flicks at the farm, never required Mom to offer him a reassuring explanation or Dad to shine a flashlight under his bed before he could fall asleep. What was it about me? Although the youngest, I was significantly bigger than Jimmy. It didn't make any sense. When asked, my mother would always answer with the best of intentions, blaming my hypersensitive imagination, saying it was just "so big" that it made it easy for me to get scared. "You're the creative one, like me," she would say with a wink. "Remember, Iain, a vivid imagination is a blessing."

I must have dozed off. I'm startled awake by a strange noise coming from outside. I'm not really sure how to explain this sound — something like a high shriek. Growing up in the country, I'm familiar with the nocturnal orchestra that performs each night, the odd sheep baaing or the customary bark of the dog. But this wasn't a dog bark. I sit up straighter and brush some curd crumbs off my chest. Maybe in my drowsy state I assumed that a sound effect from the movie had come from outside or, better yet, maybe I just imagined it altogether. I probably dreamt it.

Fuck! I hear it again. This time there's no mistaking its validity. It's coming from outside. The TV room is on the second floor and has two large windows, one at each end. I spring up and shut the drapes.

I sit back down and take a long, deep breath, peering around the room. I've never really noticed this before, but with its second-hand furniture and grandfather clock ticking away, this room is bloody creepy. I've never cared much for the collection of black-and-white headshots of Mom's grandparents and great-grandparents mounted on the wall. I examine the faces of the relatives I never knew; their colourless eyes stare back at me.

I flip deliberately through the channels until I find the soothing banter of the sports station and raise the volume several notches. I start to relax as the glib commentators review the night's Maple Leafs game. Sure, I'm living out in the secluded country now, but I used to live in the biggest city in Canada, where I walked home alone at night without fear or hesitation. I was happy to stroll through dark alleys or deserted parking garages, at all hours, without apprehension.

I'm squeezing a white line of toothpaste onto my brush when I hear the noise for a third time. It's louder now, closer. Whatever is responsible for the wail must be right outside the window, perhaps even close enough to see me. I freeze in front of the mirror, giving myself a cold stare, slowly setting the wet brush down beside the sink. The venetian blinds are open, but instead of making a move to close them I continue to stare straight ahead and remain motionless.

Only a few days earlier I spotted my first grey hair marking out territory in my beard, giving me an instant air of maturity and dignity. And now here I am, rigid as stone, too scared to close the blinds in my elderly parents' bathroom, too frightened to stay in the room with them open. I count silently to three, rinse the remnants of toothpaste into the sink, and slip quickly and quietly out the door.

I am a full-grown man, an adult. I'm twenty-seven years old, stand six feet two inches, and weigh 190 pounds. And whether I like it or not, the time for action has arrived. There's a disturbing noise coming from outside; it's not right, and it needs to be investigated. I know what I have to do. He was complaining about his sore back yesterday, but I think it's best if I wake up Dad so he can take a look outside for me. I gaze down at my feet, expecting to see the bear-claw slippers I wore as a boy.

Feeling my way down the dark hall to my parents' room, I can't help but recall the days gone by when I, the frightened little boy on his way to Dad's room for reassurance, didn't have a greying beard. I'm lost in these memories when I'm overcome by that feeling of being watched. I stop. Someone is there. I can hear soft steps behind me. A hand brushes my shoulder from behind. My heart jumps through my shirt.

"Iain," murmurs a high, creaky voice.

With nowhere to run and no brass candlestick within arm's reach, I slowly turn, accepting my fate. It's Mom, standing in her housecoat and slippers with a flashlight dangling at her side. She must have heard the noise too and is understandably seeking help. Bless her heart. I stand up straighter, reminding myself that these situations call for courage.

Mom takes a step closer and, leaning in, whispers, "I was just checking to see if you were still up, dear. I wanted to tell you to go outside and listen to the screech owls. They're all around this autumn and their mating call is marvellous."

Her yawn morphs into a grin. In the background, only steps away, I can hear Dad's rhythmic breathing.

"Yeah, they're brilliant. Actually —" I pause, looking Mom in the eye "— actually, I was just coming to tell you the same thing. I knew you'd appreciate it. You know, to us creative folk, there's nothing quite like the melodic lullaby of Mother Nature."

In the morning I wake from another turbulent sleep. I walk to the kitchen and find the empty porridge bag winking at me from the garbage.

"I think I'm going to pop down to the grocery store in a few hours. There are a few things I need," I call out to Mom, who's somewhere in the house.

It's no nature walk or therapeutic massage, but the grocery store will be my island for the afternoon. I can wander around the produce and dairy sections unnoticed. No one will know me. People stocking the shelves might see me but they won't know I'm not sleeping, and if they did they wouldn't insist I rush home to get my mandatory ten hours.

"Great," shouts Mom. "I need a couple of things too. Let me make you a small list."

She walks into the kitchen, snatches her notepad from the counter, and starts rummaging through the cupboards and refrigerator. She's a restaurant manager frantically going through the inventory for the coming weeks; I'm the seedy delivery man in a backwards baseball cap and cut-off jean shorts, waiting with my clipboard at the front door for her order. I sit down at the kitchen table. I rest my forehead against the wood, my arms dangling at my sides. The wood is cool. It feels nice.

By the time Mom finishes her "small list" it extends over the entire front side of the paper and halfway down the back. I turn it over a few times in my hands. There are several graphic sketches. It comes with verbal instructions too. *Doesn't matter what colour, just make sure to get firm olives. Only get oranges if they look like juicy ones. Do you know how to tell the juicy ones? You'll see it in their skin. And stay away from pre-sliced bread — just buy a fresh loaf and get them to slice it. Whole-grain is best, ancient grains will do.*

After three laps around, I can land a spot only at the far end of the lot. I bitterly schlep towards the grocery store, hood up, beside some guy without a jacket who's wearing a black CARPE DIEM T-shirt and has goosebumps carpeting his arms. He's talking on his cellphone. All he keeps repeating is, "Well, I told you, that's tough titty. That's just tough titty." I try to lose him but our paths seem destined to cross. Initially we both go for the same cart, and later our hands almost touch when digging for unbruised bananas.

The store is much busier and louder than I expected. I've picked a bad time. The middle of the afternoon, when the first wave of nine-to-fivers is coming in and the last few retirees are still swanning about. It's not just the chaos in the parking lot, the effort of manoeuvring my cart loutishly through the bustling produce section, or the other shoppers. Mom's list also has a hand in ruining this outing. It's ridiculously detailed and tricky to follow. I find myself squeezing and sniffing limes for ten minutes and examining endless stalks of celery to ensure I get the exact size and hue. It takes me forty-five minutes to fill the cart, and when I reach the last aisle, the only space left for the bags of milk is on the bottom rack.

If you've ever been to a grocery store at peak time, you'll know the worst is still to come. Long lines of shoppers and their hoards of pre-packaged food snake out from each cash. I don't have the energy to find the shortest, so I just head for the closest. I regret it almost instantly.

Within a few seconds I hear the sound of tapping on cardboard. I turn and see a short woman, probably in her early sixties, standing with a short man, likely her husband. Each has a full cart of groceries. The lady is impatiently drumming her nails on the Hungry Man microwaveable dinner in her cart. I'm struck by the couple's uniformity. He's only an inch taller than her, and both are heavyset and have blatantly dyed inky brown hair. They're wearing shiny windbreakers, jeans, and white sneakers. It's not a family resemblance but one brought on by years spent living together, eating the same food, breathing the same air, shopping at the same stores.

"Might be her first day," the lady says.

Her husband is quick to extrapolate. "She's taking forever." He nods towards the teenage cashier. "She just doesn't look comfortable."

"Right," I say. "A bad time to shop."

I've never loved grocery-line conversations. I fall into the unfavourable habit of judging people, not only by their appearance but also by their food choices. When I'm flagging and the strangers show an eagerness to chat, my aversion only grows. I pick up an *Archie* comic from the rack and flip through it with my back to the pair.

"You got a lot of groceries there. Lots of hungry kids at home, I bet."

"Maybe his wife's pregnant," jokes the man. "Remember how much you used to eat?"

Used to eat, I think. I turn my head slowly. "No," I say, closing the comic, "I'm not married. No kids either."

My response is inadequate. "That's a lot of food for one person."

"Well, it's for me —" I clear my throat "— and my parents."

"Your parents?" says the man. "Oh, are you still living at home?"

"You look old enough to own your own house," adds the woman. "A lot of you guys are delaying the tough choices these days. It's a generational thing. Times have changed."

From the way she's dressed, smells, talks, and stands and the frozen food melting in her cart, she strikes me as the type of woman who, when asked at a restaurant if she would care for a drink, would answer with a question of her own: "Does the fountain pop come with free refills?"

"Yup, the son of our neighbour, John, did the same thing. He moved back home after school. It's pretty common these days."

I peer towards the cashier to see how she is making out. *For the love of God, swipe faster. I don't care if you are fourteen . . . swipe, dammit!*

The woman leans in closer to her husband and bumps him with her elbow. "Course, John was studying for law school." Now she's looking back at me. "He's just graduated from law school."

"Was it law school?" wonders the man.

"Pretty sure it was. Maybe his master's, or something to do with business."

"I don't think John's graduated yet. He's definitely got one more year."

"I can remember him coming over to the house when he was five and six." Suddenly she's maudlin. "He was always so healthy; never even caught a cold."

"Yes, he's always been sturdy. And always had girls around him too, the lucky bugger," says the man.

Show me someone who doesn't believe in evolution and I will show them this man, a man so unmistakably descended from the apes I almost expect him to start picking bits of dust and dandruff from his wife's hair while she talks. His own thinning hair is slicked back, and his long arms hang limply at his sides, his hands falling well below his hips.

Our line hasn't moved. I'm starting to feel queasy. All the food isn't helping. Neither is the smell. The strength of the woman's floral perfume is matched only by its ability to induce nausea. So much so that I consider reaching into her cart and grabbing the aerosol can of cheese sitting beside her six-pack of Pepsi, inserting it into each of my nostrils, and discharging its processed contents like a caulking gun.

I'm still gazing at the cheese can when the man puts yet another question to me that I'm giddy to answer.

"So, what did you study at school? Business?"

"History," I say, breathing through my mouth, "and English."

"And what were you hoping to do with that?" the woman follows up strategically. They are well trained in their sport, this grocery-line discourse, and they play together as one.

"A university degree doesn't go nearly as far as it used to," says the man.

"We know lots of former students in debt," she says. "They're worse off in some ways than if they just started working right out of high school."

"I worked at my job for more than forty years, and I never went to university."

"But look at your hips now, Philip. You can barely walk up the stairs."

"I'm fine," he scoffs. "Just a little arthritis — one of the many charms of growing old."

I think, if I could get through this line right now, I would replace my own healthy, pain-free hips with those of Philip. In fact I'm sure I would. I would take a raging case of arthritis in my knees, ankles, both wrists, both shoulders, even my neck if I could just limp out to the car with my food in brown paper bags.

"Even with debt, I think university is still a good thing," I say. "For some people, anyway."

"I wonder if you'll feel the same if you ever have kids of your own. It all adds up."

"And hopefully for you, that will be soon," says the

woman, flashing a gaudy smile. "Just don't get discouraged."

Miraculously the line pushes ahead and it's my turn to load up the black conveyer belt. I do so madly, grabbing food out of my cart in armfuls. I'm fumbling to get my credit card out of my wallet when Philip offers his parting wisdom. "Hang in there, no matter what happens. Life goes in cycles. After the downs there's always the ups . . . usually."

I nod, collect my food, and scurry through the door, leaving the couple just as they're asking the cashier how long she's had her job.

I stand behind my car, loading the bags robotically into the trunk. It's raining. Not heavily, but trivially, closer to mist. Behind me I detect Philip and his wife wheeling out their spoils. I peek back over my shoulder. He's pushing the cart while she's chatting away. I stay where I am, my hair and shoulders going from damp to wet, and watch as they drive off.

I imagine it will be a short drive. When they get home, they'll eat dinner. And then probably read the newspaper or watch TV until one of them starts yawning and then the other, and they'll decide it's time for bed. They'll both be asleep within minutes. They won't toss or turn. There will be no time for pondering or worrying or pining, just a deep, restful, uninterrupted sleep.

Seven

Night Out

I'VE FALLEN INTO THE HABIT of evading the phone. I haven't answered it in weeks. I like to enter a conversation on my own terms, when the time is right for me. For me a ringing phone is like the whirl of a fan in summer or the intermittent hum of the furnace in winter. It's just another sound in the house, one to be ignored.

This morning I got an email from my pal Steve. He told me he was going to call me in the afternoon. He's looking for someone to grab a beer with, since he's been working long hours all week. Steve's a lawyer. "You should come into the city for a couple of hours," he wrote. "You've been back in Ottawa for half a year but you're spending all your time with your parents . . . and those animals." The last thing he wrote: "Answer the phone!"

Steve makes an interesting point. Not about the phone, but that I've been spending more and more time at Lilac Hill. I've unwittingly slipped further into a hermit's lifestyle, one that would surely have garnered praise from the late J. D. Salinger.

Sadly, it's not just my thin social life that has receded further but also my working hours. I've been picking up fewer and fewer shifts with each passing week, because I've been offered fewer and fewer shifts with each passing week. I was given only one day of work this week.

So I've just hung around the farm, mostly inside, where I have the company of not only the woodstove, which we've been using the past few days, but also the couch. It's a spot I've come to know well: my parents' ragged couch, a large window to the left, the fire directly in front. The couch doesn't pester me about much. There's no cover charge for sitting or lying on the couch, and the couch doesn't ask for two story ideas every morning. The couch doesn't judge.

No one's favourite month is November. It's too moody and indecisive. One day it tries to hold on to optimism, offering up some sun and moderate warmth, and the next day it's all grey clouds, bitter winds, and frosty lawns.

I probably should have changed. Not because I'm self-conscious about looking sloppy but because I'm wearing Dad's wool work jacket that smells of the sheep barn. I've left the couch and the farm for the first time in a couple of days. I was inspired by Steve's email. I've only come to one of those large chain bookstores, but still it's out in public.

I've just purchased a two-dollar coffee and am trying to balance it in my palm, along with my change, my wallet, my car keys, and a book. The café is already in full holiday mode. It smells of cinnamon and mint and is plastered with

Christmas banners and posters of candy canes and winter sledding scenes. Most of the patrons are elderly women sitting in twos and threes at the round wooden tables. One gentleman, who was sent back to the cash by his wife, is trying to exchange his piece of gingerbread loaf for a piece of pumpkin square. He seems bashful but firm. I'd already seen him in the washroom, coming out of one of the stalls. He seems like a different man now that he's trying to assert himself. His wife, still showing her displeasure with her first bite of gingerbread, is sitting at a table by the window, grimacing.

I'm lingering by the cream-and-sugar stand, waiting for a tray of free samples to reach me, when I feel a tap on my back. I turn slowly to see a male face I vaguely recognize.

"Iain?" says the face.

"Oh, hey." Who is this large, goateed man? Did I go to high school with him?

"I thought it was you. I haven't seen you in, like, ten years."

"At least," I reply.

I think he wants to go in for a handshake, but it's too awkward with my full hands. And how did he recognize me? I haven't shaved in three days and I'm wearing a plaid scarf, Dad's farmer's jacket, jeans with a rip in the left shin, and black rubber boots — not because rubber boots are trendy but because I carried a bale of hay to the sheep before I got into the car and drove here.

"So, are you still living around here? I thought I heard you were in Toronto."

"I was in Toronto for a few years. But yeah, I've recently moved back to the area." That's it — I know who he is.

I worked with this guy for about three months the summer I was a waiter. I think that's him . . . Yeah, it's him.

"You livin' in an apartment or a house?"

"Yeah, a house. How about you? Where are you living?"

"I'm living about three minutes away, in that new development. We bought there last year. Jill works close by, so we wanted to be in this neighbourhood."

"Nice."

"And it's near both of our parents."

"Sweet."

"And we wanted something a bit bigger. We had a kid last month. I'm still on leave. I have another week left."

"Must be busy with a baby."

"Oh, it's good times. But yeah, very busy. It's crazy."

"For sure."

"Do you have any kids?"

"Kids? Ahh, no, not yet." I respond as if I've just been asked if I want a refill on my coffee.

"Do your parents still live on that farm? Didn't they raise goats or something?"

"Yeah, they're still there. I think they might have a few animals still."

And then he lays it on me. "So, what are you up to these days? What do you do now?"

For a second I think about throwing my full cup of overpriced coffee into the air and sprinting out the double doors. "Well, I'm actually working at CBC Radio these days."

"Right on." He gives me a probing look. "And what do you do there?"

"I'm an associate producer."

He takes a sip of coffee. His eyes narrow and peer over the cup's rim at my baggy farmer's coat and mud-caked rubber boots.

"Sounds pretty slick. How did you get that?"

"Just worked my way up."

"What kind of hours is it?"

Presently it's the middle of the afternoon on a weekday. "It's all different hours; there's really no set schedule or anything. Which is good and bad, I guess."

"CBC. That's *Hockey Night in Canada*, right?"

"Yeah, I guess it is, but that's TV."

"Have you run into Don Cherry, like, in the elevator or anything?"

"No, I haven't." I've begun nodding compulsively like a bobble-head to fill any dead air.

"What about Ron MacLean? Do you ever see him around?"

"Nah, haven't met him either."

"One of these days maybe."

I can't believe I'm still nodding; I don't know how to stop.

"Well," he says, "good to see you, buddy. I gotta go find the wife and kid." He leans in, shielding his mouth with his hand. "He's probably shit his pants already."

"Huh."

"He does that better than anyone."

"Yeah?"

"And it seriously never stops. But I'm not complaining. It's good times, good times."

"I bet."

I rest my paper cup on the ground between my boots. It might just be a squeaky door hinge, but I think I can hear a baby's cry as our hands meet in a firm handshake.

When I get home, I make some tea and sit in front of the computer. There's another email from Steve. It's just a reminder about meeting up for drinks. Again he tells me to answer the phone.

When the phone rings, I'm occupied with a bowl of cereal and reading the back of the box. (I should say here that the back of a cereal box is no longer the back. The front and back are both the same; both just have the cereal's logo. I have no idea when we lost the backs of cereal boxes, but it's discouraging.) I don't bother to check the call display. I push Talk and say hello. The voice on the other end says hello. It's male, but it's not Steve.

I drop my spoon into the pool of milk. This is the first time I've spoken to a stranger in weeks. He says he represents one of the major political parties. After a thirty-second intro, in which he glibly states who he is, where he's calling from, and what a beautifully crisp day it is, he puts his opening question to me.

"So, am I speaking with Lain?"

"Excuse me?"

"Is this Lain?"

"No, it's not."

"Sorry, sir. Is Lain home?"

"There is no Lain here."

"Oh."

"I think you want Iain."

"Okay, sir. Are you Iain?"

"I am."

"Hi there, Iain. I'm terribly sorry. That's embarrassing. I apologize for getting that wrong. Someone here must have misspelled it. There's an extra I in my form here that shouldn't be there."

"No, it should."

"No, sir, they've got your name down with two I's in it. And I mistakenly read the first one as an L. My mistake, I apologize."

"But it's correct."

"So, it is an L?"

"No, it's an I."

"Um, sir?"

"I have two I's in my name."

"You have two I's in your name, like I-A-*I*-N."

"Correct."

"Really?"

"Yup. I-A-I-N."

Silence on the other end. "Wow, sir, you know, that's really beautiful. Is it Irish?"

"Scottish."

"Amazing!"

Turns out he wants money from me, whatever I can spare. I tell him, honestly, I don't have any to give. I tell him I haven't been working much lately. He still keeps me on the line for ten minutes. Ten minutes of pseudo decorum. Ten minutes of insincere observations. Ten minutes of overt cunning in the hopes of influencing me. After hearing about my limited funds, he even offers up some general life advice, touching on the obvious (and in this case, ironic) "money isn't everything" sentiment. My interaction with this guy leaves a melancholic taste in my mouth. I'm feeling less enthused about going out tonight, and even less keen about interacting with any other humans.

Back in Toronto I fancied a local pub, a short stroll from my apartment, called the Victory Café. The Victory's a cozy spot with lots of beer on tap and tasty, affordable fare. I even wrote a complimentary review of the place for an airline magazine. Sometimes I would pop by alone, but more often I would meet up with friends, either by plan or unexpectedly.

It's different at Lilac Hill. Here the local watering hole is called Little Blue. There isn't any pub food, the atmosphere is a touch draggy, and there's no service, but it's a fine spot to grab a drink. Mostly it's beer. And I'm definitely considered a regular, which is nice. Other regulars at Little Blue — also known as Dad's beer fridge — are Dad and the three black-and-white cats, which I'm getting to know much better this fall: Ma Fille, Little Miss, and Harry Snugs. Their litter box is located two feet from the small blue fridge, so they're regulars by default. I often watch them paw through the granular litter while I'm pouring my cold beer into a glass.

"Sorry, Little Miss," I'll say, dropping the empty bottle back into the case, my T-shirt pulled up over my mouth and nose. "I'll be out of your way in just a sec."

Little Miss will continue glaring at me as she digs around, waiting for some privacy. Like me, the three black-and-white cats are spending more time indoors with the changing season. It's only Pumpkin, the orange cat, who's still holding firm outside until the first snow.

When Steve calls, an hour later, I let him go to the machine to make sure it's him. I call him back and tell him about my reservations. I tell him how I don't like November, it's windy outside, my car hasn't been running well, I think the exhaust is broken, it's embarrassingly loud. He's persistent. After a few minutes I've agreed to meet him downtown at a pub called the Manx.

"Shall we say 10 p.m.?"

"We shall."

Mom and Dad have made dinner together: fresh bread, lasagna, and salad. The lasagna still has another hour to bake. I'm standing in front of the oven, enjoying the aroma. Mom comes up behind me and asks for a hand outside. She's relocating her potted herbs from the back deck to a reserved spot inside, in front of a west-facing window.

"They still like the sunlight," she says.

Mom's role is door opener and navigator. I am the grunt. She directs me to the herbs. I pick them up (making sure to bend my legs, as directed by Mom) and lug them into the house. The pots are large and full of earth, so I carry only one a time.

"Okay, take a left through the laundry room," Mom's shouting behind me, "and watch you don't trip on the tile. It just goes from carpet to tile without warning."

"Yes, yes, I know, Mom."

First it's the rosemary, followed by the thyme, basil, lemon basil, and sage. I follow Mom back outside, where there's only one pot left on the deck. I see the barn light has been switched on. Dad must be in there.

"He looks kinda sad, doesn't he," says Mom.

"What?"

"Sad," repeats Mom.

"Do you mean the cilantro?"

"No, but yes."

"What?"

"It's not cilantro, it's parsley. But yes, the parsley looks lonely."

"I thought maybe you meant Dad. What's he doing in the barn?"

"No, he's not sad, I'm sure he's happy to be taggin' the sheep. I bet he'd love some help."

"My help?"

"Sure. I'd do it, but I'm clearly not going to be much of a help with taggin'."

I take a step back, bringing my hand up to my chest. "What's Dad doing to our sheep?"

"Taggin' them." The ridiculous phrase sinks in after she says it for the third time, sounding out each word carefully. Mom buckles over in a fit of laughter. She covers her mouth with both hands. "Oh, my . . . tagging the girls . . ."

When her laughter subsides, she explains that Dad is giving the sheep their ear tags.

"Do you need any more herb help?" I ask.

"No, it's just the parsley left. You can go help Dad," Mom says, giggling again. "I can handle the lonely parsley."

I find Dad standing over one of the sheep. He's holding one with his hip against the barn wall and has his ear-piercing contraption in his right hand. I don't say anything but watch from the door as he brings the instrument up to her ear, steadies it, and squeezes down. He backs away and the ewe runs to the other side of the barn with her new ear tag.

Dad's tagging the sheep because it's required by law if they are taken off the property. Each tag has a number on it to keep the animals in order. That's why Marshall's our only sheep with a proper name. He's the only permanent resident; the rest are just numbers. This system is clearly meant for larger farms that have herds numbering in the hundreds or thousands. We have Marshall and eight permanent ewes, and we take only a few lambs away in the truck each year, either to slaughter or for sale. As far as I know there's no plan to take any others off the property, but still Dad complies.

"Need a hand?" I ask.

Dad turns abruptly. "Sure. I only have a couple more to do."

Dad's able to catch each one and wrestle and hold it still against the wall. He gets me to load the metal device with the ear tag and pass it to him when he's ready. I don't feel like much of a help, but still he thanks me when we're done.

"Do you think those ear tags hurt the sheep?" I ask.

"No. It probably hurts my back a lot more."

"You need any more help?"

"I'm just going to check on the ducks. You can go on in."

Dinner won't be ready for another few minutes, and since I haven't been outside much in the last couple of weeks,

I take my time making my way back to the house. I pass by the magnolia tree Dad planted around the time I moved home. It still isn't looking too dapper. I run my hand along one of the thin branches. It feels almost hollow, and it looks the same as it did when I first saw it — skinny, frail, delicate, and free of any blooms or leaves. It's a brown skeleton.

On my way into town I'm listening to the AM oldies station. I'm driving fast, weaving in and out of traffic. I have the volume jacked up and I'm drumming my index fingers on the wheel, using the dashboard as my hi-hat. I'm singing along with the Carpenters and don't notice the police cruiser parked along the side of the highway until it's too late. I step on the brake and reassert my grip at ten and two. I even regulate my posture, as if sitting up straighter might garner some sympathy from the cop. I keep checking the rear-view mirror, but he never pulls out to follow me. Maybe it's a good omen. *Must be my lucky night*, I think.

When I get to the pub, Steve is waiting for me. He's ordered two pints and has made it through an inch or so of his own. I sit down, draping my coat over the back of the chair. We clink our glasses and say, "Cheers." We chat about common friends, acquaintances, what everyone's been up to. I've fallen out of the loop. I hadn't realized how many of our old friends are engaged.

"Even Blackwell?" I say.

"Of course Blackwell. They've been together forever."

"Yeah, I suppose so."

"So how are things at work?" Steve asks.

"Not bad," I say, taking a swig of beer. "Not great."

"No?"

"Well, I don't I know. There's just not a lot of work to speak of these days."

"So what have you been up to?"

"I'm not sure. I've been trying to do a bit of writing."

We both gulp. "What about you, though?" I ask, hiding a burp behind my hand. "What's life like for a lawyer?"

"Good," he says, "but busy. It's nutty. I'm working like mad."

Midway through our third round of beers, I notice Steve squinting in the direction of two girls putting on their coats to leave. "Who're you looking at?" I ask.

"I know the taller one from when I used to go to camp."

As Steve replays his camp days back in his mind, the tall girl notices him. As she walks to the table I notice she's even taller than she appeared from across the room, and heavily made up. Her dark hair hangs loosely around her shoulders, except for her bangs, which have been clipped back. She arrives at our table open-mouthed and wide-eyed.

"Steve?! What are you doing here?"

"Just having a drink. How are you doing, Karen?"

"I'm great . . . We were just about to leave, but would you guys mind if I pulled up a chair?"

"Not at all," says Steve.

"I'm Iain." I wave.

Karen's friend can't be convinced to stay. It's late and she has breakfast plans in the morning. Karen, undaunted, hugs her friend, pulls up a chair, and orders another glass of red. She immediately starts to tell us about her career, but staying focused on her sermon is impossible. I can't stop staring at the maroon coating caked on her lips. They look like the surface of Mars. I wonder how many glasses she's had. Five? Seven? She's not drunk, but she's definitely not sober. She's lurching unsteadily along that line between the two.

Karen is a nurse. She's been working at it for a couple of years now. And she really, really loves it. She spends her days helping people — how could she not like it?! But she hates that the clinic she works at has a reputation for caring only for rich people. But she really, really loves being a nurse. Karen releases only a handful of trusted words from her stable (*literally*, *amazing*, and *seriously* are three of her favourites) but she's still remarkably prolix, pausing only to sip from her glass.

"So, Steven, last I heard you had just, like, graduated from law school. What firm are you at?"

Steve tells her the name of the law firm he works at. He's told her twice already. I listen to a third description of his firm. I'm sitting on my hands, my legs bouncing. "That's great, it's really great," she's saying, and then turns her wobbly gaze to me. "What is it you do again?"

"Me? Oh, not too much," I offer.

"I don't care if you're not a lawyer. Seriously, it doesn't matter."

I'm not sure what to say and think about making something up. I don't want to say I'm an associate producer anymore. It requires too much explanation. I don't want to explain how I've worked only one shift this week. I don't want to say I'm a journalist. Journalists work more than once a week. So I tell her I'm a farmer, that I keep sheep, chickens, ducks, and cats. Steve chokes on his beer. Karen's eyes are glassy and remind me of very tiny, shallow swimming pools.

"A real farmer. So do you, like, farm *and* kill your animals too?"

"Not me personally, but we do eat our own meat."

"No, I think that's totally fine. Don't worry."

"Okay."

"So, like, there's nothing to be ashamed of."

"No."

"But seriously, that's great? Seriously. And, like, do you like that?"

"Yeah, I enjoy it."

We all sip from our glasses.

"But Iain's also into writing," says Steve.

"Writing? Oh, really? What kind of writing?"

"Well, nothing too exciting, mostly just little stories or essays —"

"Do you write much for papers or magazines?"

"No."

"Well, there are so many writers out there. My idea is that someone needs to write a book about writing, like a guidebook . . . for writers . . . about writing . . . by a writer."

"Interesting."

"You should do it; it would sell."

"True."

"Sometimes I just feel ashamed that I work at the clinic I work at. Everyone always thinks it's the fancy one, and then I feel like I have to justify it. But I shouldn't have to. My patients need me where I am, just as much as they would at any other clinic. Poor, rich — patients are patients. I literally hate having to justify it, but I feel like I do. And I literally love the work."

Steve and I nod in unison.

"I've also spent a week each summer the last couple of years working at a camp for developmentally challenged kids. And it's amazing. They are so amazing. And it literally feels so amazing to know you've changed their lives for the good."

"Would you ever consider doing that type of work full time?" wonders Steve.

"No, it's always hard at the end of the week when they leave and, well, you know, go back to their lives, which are basically, like, hopeless."

Steve and I look at each other. Karen looks at Steve and then at me.

"Now, what is it that you do again?"

It feels like we've been listening to Karen all night, all the next day, and all night again. It's probably been more like twenty or thirty minutes. The pub has grown busier, and thus warmer and louder. Everyone has raised their voices a notch or two. Not Karen. She hasn't noticed. I have to concentrate to make out her words. As I do I can't help but wonder what's going on back at Little Blue. Little Miss must be basking in the rare spell of privacy.

There's a burst of loud, excessive laughter from two tables over. Another group has ordered a couple of plates of fries for the table. At least I think that's what they're eating. It smells like fries and vinegar.

"So, do you live out there with your partner?" asks Karen.

"No."

"You're not married yet?"

"Nope."

"So you're out there alone?"

"No."

"Who do you live with then? Girlfriend?"

"No. No girlfriend."

"Who?'

"Um, my parents; it's actually their farm."

"Your parents?! Really, well, that's okay. Who cares? You aren't *that* old. It doesn't matter. Do you guys get along?"

"No, we hate each other."

"That's great. I love my parents. We get along really well too. We're really close. They're getting old though. It's kinda scary but totally cute."

"Definitely."

Steve pushes his chair back and rises abruptly. "Sorry, guys, I'll be right back. Just have to use the facilities."

In this moment I loathe Steve with a murderous passion. I want to grab his arm and force him back down in his seat. Pee in a pint glass or use my toque, just don't leave me! Karen and I sit, sipping our drinks continuously. Her sips are generous and unselfconscious. Mine are trivial and nervous.

"Okay, mister," she says, "now tell me more. What else don't I know about you?"

I am a deer in the headlights. I am a child being caught with a stolen cookie in his coat pocket. I'm an old, white-haired man falling asleep on the couch after supper. I'm at a loss. "Well," I offer, "there's my name. My name is spelled differently. I spell Iain with two I's."

Karen downs the last of her wine and sets her empty glass down firmly on the table. "Oh, who cares, though? I don't think that matters at all. Who cares?" She tilts her head to the right and leans in a little closer, close enough that I can smell her Merlot-infused breath. And she places her hand softly, sympathetically atop mine. "Some things are just messed up. I-A-I-N, huh? Yeah, it is weird, but in a good way."

Karen's right. Some things are messed up. When I first came back home, I was returning temporarily, to present a book review. That turned into more work: journalism. That seems to have been a short run too. I'm starting to feel as if I'm in a giant game of snakes and ladders, only the board I'm playing on seems devoid of ladders. On my board there are only snakes.

Instead of a third pint, my next round comes in the form of syrupy fountain pop. I've decided not to crash at Steve's as we'd planned. It was Karen who'd mentioned the storm that's forecast for morning. Steve confirmed that snow and high winds are supposed to start sometime before dawn. Without proper snow tires, there's no reason to chance it. My car and the inclement weather are on unfriendly terms. I should drive back tonight while it's still clear. That means no more beer.

So while my tablemates become a little drunker, I become a little more sober. I pan from Karen to Steve and back to Karen. I zoom in close, watching their mouths move, forming words and laughter. I'm saying less than before, my contributions devolving into mere nods. I stab at the ice and extract my Coke through a straw.

After we finish our drinks, Steve offers to pay the bill. Karen doesn't let him pay for her. I let him pay for me. We all pull on our coats and shuffle outside. For a moment we stand awkwardly along the lines of an invisible isosceles triangle.

"Well, it was great to see you, Steve," Karen says, tilting her head back to zip up her jacket, "because it's been too long." They hug and Karen stumbles off towards "a slice of veggie 'za!"

My car is in the opposite direction, as is Steve's apartment, so we walk together.

"You sure you don't want to crash?" he asks when we reach my car. "You're welcome to the guest bed."

"Nah, thanks, man. I should get home. Don't want to be on the roads in the morning."

"Fair enough."

"Thanks for the beers, though," I say. "And the Coke."

"No worries. Maybe we can meet up again next weekend?'

"Yeah, maybe."

"Alright, see you."

"Later."

I unlock my door, get in, and twist the key in the ignition. The radio blares on. I immediately turn it off. As I wait for the engine to warm, I watch Steve walk along the sidewalk ahead of me, his hands tucked into his pockets.

About forty minutes later I've left the city and have exited the main highway. I'm back on a deserted country road. There are no pedestrians this far out, no store signs or building lights or gas stations, not even streetlights. There must be clouds in the sky, because the moon and stars, usually brighter out here, have been given the night off. I'm the last car on the road.

I flip the headlights off and am consumed by the darkness around me, swallowed up in a single bite. It feels as if I'm driving with my eyes closed. It's snowing now. The days aren't just getting colder but shorter too, and the nights longer. There will be less daylight tomorrow than there was today. And there will be even less the day after that.

Winter

Eight

I'll Be Home
for Christmas

WITH DECEMBER PLAYING HOST, winter has arrived, settling in unapologetically. The cats have primarily moved inside. They still enjoy the odd sniff of the outdoors but only for a few minutes at a time. With four cats you can easily get stuck in the inflaming cycle of opening and closing the door for them. They exit and enter at various times, and a whoosh of frigid air scurries in with them.

Right now it's Harry Snugs who's outside, clinging to the screen by all four sets of claws. He looks like one of those spread-eagled fuzzy cat ornaments that people stick to their car windows with suction cups. I'm sitting in the rocking chair watching him, shaking my head and frowning because I let him out only four minutes ago. I'll get up and let him in soon. I just want Harry Snugs to know that I was not put on this earth to be his personal doorman.

Last year we had one of those rare green Christmases

at the farm. I was home for only four or five days. My brother and I spent the afternoon of Christmas Eve in shorts, tossing a Frisbee in the front orchard. Not this year. We've already had several days of flurries and a heavy storm; a traditional white Christmas is a certainty. Mom's thrilled.

I'd forgotten how unarmed the old walls of the farmhouse are against the winter wind. Apart from the four-foot radius directly surrounding the woodstove, the house has become bitterly cold. The reality of the season has struck me with a second actuality: I've officially lost the only official title I've ever held. I'm no longer an associate producer, or a journalist of any kind. At least I don't think I am. Nothing has been stated formally, but I haven't been offered any more shifts in the new year. The producer I originally covered for has been back for several weeks. That really did it. It's as if I were playing a game of musical chairs all fall, and now the music has stopped and all the chairs are full.

So this year I'm uncertain how long my Christmas break will extend. I have no commitments in January. None in February. I haven't been asked about my availability. I wasn't told "See you in the new year" as I walked out after my last unmemorable shift. If I had a business card printed up right now, I suppose to be accurate it would say IAIN REID: FELINE PORTER. Maybe I could get a small cat-paw print in one of the corners.

I get up from the rocking chair and straighten my shoulders, holding my sweater together at the front as I open the door. Harry Snugs sprints by me without acknowledgement and heads for the kitchen and his bowl of kibble.

Christmas is a mere three weeks away, and there's only one week left before my sister, Jean; her stepdaughter, Loa; her husband, Johannes; and their new baby, George, arrive from Iceland. It's not that I've committed their itinerary to heart or have their arrival date marked on my calendar — Mom's been doing that for me. Whenever any version of "I'll Be Home for Christmas" starts playing, Mom stops what she's doing and reminds me (and Dad if he's around) when everyone's arriving. "I'm getting so excited," she says, running over to turn up the volume a notch or two and snapping her fingers. "Only one day and one week until a full house again." Dad and I look at each other, raise our eyebrows, and go back to whatever it is we're eating or reading.

For the past few days Mom and Dad have been busy preparing the house, stocking up on food and gifts. In almost thirty years I've never known Dad to be careless when it comes to his own purchases, even at Christmas. He rarely buys anything for himself, and when he does — even if it's just a book or tie — he deliberates over the purchase for anywhere from a week to a decade or so. So I'm agog when Dad announces he's bought himself an early Christmas present.

He doesn't seem overly excited about his news. "Come here, it's in my study. I suppose I better show you." His tone suggests he's bought himself a gift certificate for a colonoscopy.

I follow him into his study. The walls are lined with old books, and only the brass desk lamp with the green shade is lighting the room. Dad passes over a small black backpack he's just pulled from a plastic bag. I take it from him.

"Do you really think you should be spoiling yourself like this, Dad?"

"I don't know. I just thought maybe it would be easier to carry my computer and papers. Although I'm still not sure."

"It probably will be. And that briefcase of yours is ancient; it was time for something new."

"Well, I don't know," he says. "I'm not sure what it all means, me walking around the university wearing a backpack." He's talking as if *backpack* is a synonym for *prom dress*.

"Have you tried it out yet?"

"No. I have to go collect some essays on Thursday. I'll try it out then."

"It'll be a big day for you."

"Well, we'll see if I can go through with it."

"You know, Dad, it's almost apocalyptic."

"You're right," he says. "It surely is."

"Good King Wenceslas" has come on again. It's the third time I've heard it today. I get it — everything is deep and crisp and even. We're sitting around the living room when the conversation turns to a recurring topic: whether it's time for Mom to finally get herself a computer. I'm reading the paper, munching on a handful of holiday snacking nuts, listening idly to Mom and Dad's conversation.

"I'm just not sure I want to get into that whole realm." The realm Mom's referring to is that of the Internet and email.

"I know," says Dad, "but you won't be able to hold out forever." He's flipping through a glossy catalogue, calling Mom over whenever he comes across a good deal.

"That's true," answers Mom, peering over his shoulder, "but I was hoping to keep putting it off."

"But now's the time."

"Why?"

"Because there are some good Christmas deals. But more important, because Iain's still around. He can show you how to use it."

I choke on a roasted chestnut before spitting it into my hand. I've seen Mom struggle with electronics before. Teaching her to use a computer is about as appealing as finding myself under the mistletoe with a lovesick Lucius. Mom's just not a computer type, the same way Dad avoids the dance floor at weddings. In fact, she's never even used one. For her it's not just a big step but an entire staircase — a long, steep spiral staircase.

"That's true. Iain seems to know computers well," says Mom.

"I bet it'll be fun," says Dad. "Now he can pay you back for teaching him to ride a bike."

It's true. Mom did teach me how to ride a bike. But unlike most who learn, I wasn't four or five or even six. Mom waited until I was thirteen before teaching me. It was, unfortunately, the same summer as my biggest growth spurt. I was undeniably gawky at six feet tall and was just starting to experience the unflattering kiss of acne. Mom drove me to a busy park in the heart of the city. It was there that she ran along beside her gangly teenage son, supporting his back with one hand and holding the seat of the rusty bike with the other. She kept me in the park until after dark that night, yelling encouragement through fall after fall.

Our comedic display brought about groups of hecklers, and they too were unwavering. But today I can ride a bike, and I suppose I owe her for that. Still, I'm not ready to give in without a fight.

"What's the rush?" I plead. "It can waste a lot of time. Are you sure you're ready for email, Mom?"

"If I was any older I probably wouldn't bother, but —"

"Well, you're already in your sixties, for heaven's sake," I say. "You're not exactly a spring chicken. So it's understandable if you never learn . . . plus it's going to be busy the next few weeks, with everyone coming home for Christmas."

"That's just it. She has the motivation to learn," says Dad, putting a hand on Mom's knee, "now that she's a grandma."

"I know, you're absolutely right. But I'm still a little torn. There are so many things to waste time on already," says Mom.

A week or two later a box with the blue Dell logo stamped on the side arrives at the farm. I walk into the kitchen knowing that my afternoon is ruined. The sight of Mom's new computer has hit me like a kick in the groin.

"Hey, Mom —"

She raises her hand in response. "Just a sec, I'm listening to this story on the radio."

I wait until the reporter has signed off before asking her to clarify. "What was that all about?"

"It's just awful," she says. "Some guy froze his mom's body after she died so he could keep cashing her monthly pension cheques. Talk about sick. What a story to hear around the holidays."

"Pretty weird," I agree. "Although in fairness, didn't you freeze Tramp in the freezer for, like, a year after he died?"

Tramp was our beloved family dog, the smartest, friendliest, proudest animal I've ever encountered. After he died at the ripe age of fourteen, Mom and Dad kept him buried in the box freezer, waiting for the weather to change so they could cremate him on a specially constructed bonfire and bury the ashes on the hill where he used to lie. Theoretically I understood the plan, but Tramp stayed in the freezer for more than seven months.

"That's different; the weather stayed cold later than usual that year. Besides, I wasn't cashing any cheques on Tramp's behalf."

"No, but he was my best friend growing up — and I found his rigid body wrapped in blankets and a pillowcase when I went to get an ice-cream sandwich."

"Poor Trampy, he was such a great dog," Mom says. "You know, after all this, I don't feel like getting started on that computer anymore. And I was so excited this morning. I need to be motivated."

"Well, why did you keep listening to that ridiculous story? You hushed me when I came in."

"I know. But you know me: once I start listening I can't stop."

It takes me more than an hour to convince Mom we should start her first tutorial. I could have kept her going down the opposite path, which I seriously considered, talking about frozen mothers and frozen pets, knowing these images would put her in a sour mood, leaving her with no energy or incentive to start on the computer. But as much as I'm dreading it — and I am — I know that the longer we put it off, the more it will dominate my thoughts. I'm going with the old-fashioned Band-Aid approach: let's just close our eyes and rip the damn thing off, as quickly and painlessly as possible. Still, this isn't going to be a jaunt; it's going to be a journey. I set a full pot of coffee to brew.

First I show Mom how to turn the computer on. She does so without incident. A better start than I'd anticipated.

"Okay," I say, "now try moving the cursor to the top icon."

"Perfect," she replies. "What's the cursor?"

"Right," I say. "I didn't mean to move so . . . fast. The cursor is that little arrow. Just imagine it as an extension of your hand."

"They should make it a little finger, then, not some arrow. One small index finger would do the trick. It would be much clearer."

"Well, the arrow isn't all that murky, Mom. Everyone has already kinda agreed on it."

"I'm just saying, a finger would be better . . ." She holds a single straight finger up beside the computer.

"*Anyway*, try moving the arrow to that top icon that says 'My Documents.'"

"You got it," she says.

I watch the screen intently but nothing happens. The cursor remains painfully static. I do, however, sense a flurry of activity beside me. I turn to see Mom staring at the screen, holding the mouse up off the table and moving it around in tiny clockwise circles like a maestro gripping a baton.

"The arrow isn't moving," she says, biting her lip in

concentration. "It's not going up . . . it's not going anywhere."

It takes some time, but I finally get Mom to understand the physical limitations of her computer. With extreme trepidation we wade into the waters of the Internet. I get her to open a web browser. "Just double-click on the icon there, the one that says 'Firefox.'"

She's not graceful with the mouse but is eventually able to land the arrow overtop the icon and methodically execute a shaky double-click.

"Now what?" she asks, brushing some hair off her forehead.

"We might as well get you an email address. What do you want it to be?"

Mom rests her hand on her chin. "I've got it," she says. "I love the big bear." The bear she's referring to is Dad. A charming idea, sure, but completely unrealistic.

"I don't think that'll work, Mom. There's already so many email addresses out there, and remember, you'll be giving this out to everyone, not just family."

"Just try it," she demands.

I do. It's already taken. So Mom, undaunted, tries again. "How about whistlewhileyouwork?" she says.

"Mom, that's not going to work either." But she isn't listening; instead she's whistling over my negativity, waving her hands with the tune.

I try it. Whistlewhileyouwork is already taken. We continue this stultifying dance, going back and forth for half an hour. She insists I try each suggestion. Pumpkinismycat. Attitudeiseverything. Thepeterpanfan. Each one is rejected. Then mercifully we land on one that's available, and Mom settles reluctantly on it. "I guess it'll have to do for now," she says. "It's not as good as the others, but it was my nickname in elementary school, so I can remember it."

"It'll do just fine. It's a great choice, Mom," I lie.

Although she won't be sending or receiving any emails for a while, next, on Dad's request, I prepare Mom for looming threats. I log into my own account and show her an email in my junk box from a Nigerian fellow named Joseph, claiming to be royalty and promising riches if I send him some money to help secure his release from prison. "These are the things to avoid, Mom. Any emails about money or bank account numbers. They're all scams. Delete them right away."

She looks at me gravely. "Are there people who just sit around all day thinking of ways to use their computers to scam people?"

"Unfortunately that's the reality, Mom."

"Well," she says, "I feel sorry for Joseph."

"Don't be. He's probably the same guy who froze his mom. He probably did it 'cause she couldn't figure out the Internet." I realize how grim this must sound to Mom and instantly regret saying it.

"Yeah," she says, wistfully, "you're probably right. So many twisted people out there, and I'll never get the hang of this either."

We sit in defeated silence, wilting over her computer. She may never bother to learn now. The computer will be relegated to the same fate as the nugatory juicer and compact exercise machine, both growing old and dusty on the shelves in the basement. Sure, it would have taken several long, agonizing weeks — more likely months — to learn, but she would have got the hang of it . . . eventually. There was so much potential. She could have learned to email, specifically to her grandson in Iceland. She could have reconnected with some old university friends. She could have uploaded pictures from her camera. She could even have started writing more poetry. But now, who knows? Maybe my flippant remark has demoralized her for good. I look over at Mom. She's clearly discouraged.

"Well," she says, "there's one thing I feel like doing now."

"Come on, it takes everyone a few tries to get comfortable. You don't want to give up just yet, do you?"

"What? No, I'd really love to make a prank call . . . Can we use this thing to alter my voice?"

"What?" I gasp. "You want to make a crank call? Now?"

"Course," she says, perking up. "I remember you used to do that when you were away at school. I've had a great one planned for Grandma that I've been meaning to try out. You'll just need to show me where to talk."

"Okay, I guess I'll grab the phone." It's a good thing she's come around, I think. The computer really is going to open up a whole new world for Mom.

"So you'll make my voice sound like a middle-aged man's, right? A smoker would be best."

"Ah, yeah, I can do that."

As I pull my chair closer to the table, handing the phone to Mom, I'm thankful Dad isn't around to see us use this beautiful new machine to prank-call Grandma. Outside it's started snowing again.

"This'll be great," she says, her eyes widening. "It's almost Christmas — she'll never suspect a thing!"

It's the last day before the Icelandic invasion. Dad's returned home with a pine tree strapped into the box of his truck with bungee cords. I watch him drive carefully up the lane. It's a big tree; the thick branches reach over the roof and spill out the back hatch. When he enters the kitchen, it looks as if he's been dusted with icing sugar. His cheeks are cherry red.

"I made another Christmas purchase this afternoon," he says while unwinding his scarf.

"Saw you driving in, Dad."

"Oh, so you know about the tree."

"I do."

"I can't believe it'd been passed over. It was the nicest tree on the lot, no question. I hope it looks good inside; you never know."

"Well, don't worry, Mom doesn't know about it yet. You can still surprise her."

"I hope she likes it," he says, kicking snow off his black boots. "You just never know."

The arrival of the Christmas tree is my notice of eviction from the family room. I leave Dad to his tree-raising duty and move my books, papers, and computer up to my bedroom. Mom stops me in the hall outside my room. She informs me that they think it's best for Jean, Johannes, and the baby to sleep in my room, on account of the layout and the larger bed.

"I guess I should move my stuff into Jean's old room, then?" I ask.

"No, that won't work either. Loa, Jean's teenage step-daughter, is going to be sleeping in there."

I carry my stuff back downstairs to the chilly storage room and the pullout couch. In a certain beneficial way it makes me feel that I too am just visiting for Christmas.

"I just can't get over it," Mom's saying. We've joined Dad in the family room. We've strung the lights, embedded the silvery tinsel throughout the branches, placed some candy canes near the trunk, and have moved on to the decorations, which are kept in four cardboard boxes. All of the ornaments are wrapped separately in white tissue paper. Like the house decorations, they haven't changed. They're the same ones my parents have been hanging on pine trees for forty years.

"It really is a beautiful tree," she says.

"I wasn't sure you were going to like it," Dad confesses. "I went with my gut. What do you think, Iain?"

They look at me.

"About what?"

"The tree."

"Sure, I like the tree," I answer, freeing my third candy cane from its plastic wrap.

"How could you not? It's a wonderful tree," says Mom.

"Yeah, it's a decent tree," I say.

"Oh, it's more than just decent," counters Mom.

"It is a fairly impressive tree, Iain. Seeing it up, I'm quite happy with it," says Dad.

"It fits the space just perfectly," says Mom. "And I love the smell!"

Dad had trimmed the bottom, carried the tree inside, and held it in place while I brought the red stand out of its case, guiding the base of the trunk into its grip. Dad's not much of a decorator, tree or otherwise, so with the selection, purchase, and transportation of the tree to the house, his work was done for the evening. He watches this final chapter unfold from his armchair.

In the time I hang five or six decorations, Mom hangs one. With each she asks if I remember it and then recounts an accompanying anecdote. "Oh, do you remember this one, Iain? The hand-carved Rudolph; I've always loved this Rudolph. We got it in a craft shop in England." She hangs Rudolph on the tree, steps back, and then re-hangs him another ninety-three times until she's found the exact branch that suits the ornament.

Sometimes she's able to find a more suitable spot for the ones I've hung too. "Sorry," she whispers, "that area just had one too many; seemed a tad busy."

"What about the lights? Should we plug them in, see how they look?" I ask.

"What? No." Dad leans forward in his chair. "You know the rules, bud. We have to wait until the end to turn the lights on, until everything's up."

"Lights are the last thing," says Mom. "The rules are the rules."

Having been reminded of the tenets, I continue until all of the boxes are empty. Tissue paper litters the coffee table and floor.

"That's it," declares Mom, running her hand through the last empty box.

"Okay, I'll get the nog." Dad's up, retreating to the fridge to fetch our drinks. He returns with three glasses. "A little fresh nutmeg on top," he says, winking as he passes them out.

Dad places his on a coaster beside his seat and crawls into position behind the tree. Mom cuts the ceiling lights as Dad plugs in the tree. To my surprise, none of the bulbs are burnt out.

"Look at that," says Dad, peering up from his knees. "Not too shabby."

"Wow, beautiful," adds Mom. "I think it's the best tree we've ever had."

On cue, as she does every year at this moment, Mom sits on the maroon couch and starts singing "O Christmas Tree." After singing this song for more than thirty years, she's still familiar with only the first few lines. She hums the rest discordantly. "Come on, Iain, join in anytime."

Dad's buried his face in his chest, chortling. He brings up his hands, rubbing his eyes. "After all these years and all these trees, you still don't know the words."

Mom grins, shoos his comments away with a swat of her hand, and continues humming. "Come on, Iain, you can hum, can't you?" says Mom.

"Not really," I say. I'm sitting in the chair opposite Dad, sideways, my legs hanging over the armrest.

"You can whistle, though," says Dad. "I remember you used to whistle all the time."

"Let's just keep it as is. Carry on, Mom. No one wants to hear whistling."

My comment causes her to stop abruptly. "Don't be silly. We'd love to hear some whistling. It's a great idea."

"Let's hear some, then," exclaims Dad.

It's difficult now for us to see each other clearly through the glow of the tree lights. It's easier to look out the large windows facing the orchard. The snow outside is deep and swirls around in the wind. Mom shushes the already quiet room. I inhale and start whistling "O Christmas Tree." Mom and Dad both lean back and cross their feet at the ankles. They're listening intently, as if they're being treated to a live orchestral performance of *The Nutcracker*. I finish my first and only verse.

"That's a real talent you have," claims Mom.

"Yes, and a useful one too," I point out.

Dad sips from his glass mindfully. "Including that flurry of warbles made it sound altogether different. Nicely done."

Mom doesn't stay seated for long; she's spreading out a white sheet under the tree. "I almost forget about the sheet."

"You can't forget that," says Dad. "That's where the presents go."

"That reminds me, I hope you've held up your end of the deal this year. I really don't need any presents from you. You know that." She's looking pointedly at Dad now.

"I know, I know," he says, holding his hands up in the air. "Same for me. We've agreed, no presents for each other this year."

"I'm going back to the kitchen. Anyone ready for a refill?" I ask.

Both glasses are raised. I accept them in one hand.

"Nutmeg," says Dad. "Don't forget the nutmeg."

I can't believe that five of us were living here for all those years. There were fights (both physical and verbal) and dis-agreements, but we managed to endure. My sister, Jean, and her family have been at the farm for only three days, and the house is — well, the house is full again, like it was when we were growing up.

I'd grown accustomed to the tranquil routine of three people at the farm, two of whom are seniors. Adding a thirteen-year-old girl and a three-month-old lad, along with the steady parade of dogs and cats, has created a feeling of city life within the house. There are lines for the bathroom, the toaster, even to read the newspaper in the morning. Meal-times in the kitchen are the equivalent of rush hour, with people standing behind one another at the fridge, bumping knees under the table, fighting for the last piece of bacon. Once word spread that Jean is back from Europe and *has the baby with her*, neighbours have been stopping by in bunches.

Jean and Johannes were married here at the farm, and the neighbours played a significant role in the festivities, housing Johannes's friends and relatives, preparing food, and hosting parties. One of the local farmers even spent the afternoon before the wedding driving up and down the road picking up any roadkill so the area would look nicer for the out-of-town guests. So Mom and Jean are both pleased to see any of the neighbours. It doesn't matter if it's planned or a drop-in, they'll always have time for them. Tea is served, cookies are consumed, and photographs are pored over on Jean's computer.

My brother, Jimmy, has driven in from the city after work to visit every night this week. He's eaten dinner with us and has built an ice rink beside the duck pond. He's even fastened a floodlight to one of the elm trees for night skat-ing. We teach Loa how to skate. She's pretty good. We try to teach Johannes how to play hockey, but he prefers to slide along the bumpy ice in his boots, steadying himself with the stick.

Right now Dad and Johannes are outside shovelling snow, Loa's watching a movie, and Mom's wrapping gifts. I'm sitting at the dining-room table with Jean, playing cribbage. George is sitting inertly in her lap. I've never beaten Jean at cribbage. Or, come to think of it, at any game that requires wit, knowledge, or quick thinking. Considering our different personalities and interests, Jean and I have always got along well. She left home for university when I was only twelve or thirteen, and then four years later she moved overseas. For the past fifteen years I've seen her only a couple of times a year.

"Can you hold the baby for a minute?" she asks.

I look up from my cards. "Me?"

I kept hearing how amazing it was going to be to have a new baby around for Christmas. *It'll be so much fun! It'll be so great for you! You're an uncle now! You'll finally be able to do uncle stuff!!!* So far baby George drools a fair amount, sleeps a lot, and drinks milk, which he may or may not spit back up onto his minuscule shirt. Sometimes he cries. And he wakes up throughout the night, either to drink more milk or to cry, or both. From the foam pullout in the storage room directly underneath, I can hear him lucidly.

"Just for a second."

"Your baby?"

"Here, take him." She hands me the gelatinous pink mound she calls her son. I handle him uncertainly, as if she's passed me a sandbag with a hole in it. I grip him rigidly under the armpits, not sure what to do about the leaking sand. It's an unflattering position for George, his chin rippling into three fleshy disks. He reminds me of a piecrust that's been taken out of the oven a few minutes too soon. I can't really tell what he's going to look like; his human form hasn't quite set in. I'm grinning foolishly. I'm a clown without a costume, a jester without his hat. Every so often George twitches or extends an arm upward or a leg outward. We're locked in the nervous pose of teenage slow dancers: touching, barely, and neither owning enough nerve to breach the two-foot gap. He's drooling from the left side of his mouth and making gurgling noises. The muscles around my mouth are sore from holding this silly grin. Some of his drool manages to find an area of exposed skin on my left wrist and thumb. I quickly wipe it on his shirt.

When Jean returns, I'm echoing his alien noises like an auditory mirror. She wonders how we got on.

"Swimmingly," I reply. "Like a couple of old friends."

It's Christmas Eve. It might actually be Christmas by now. It's late. We had tourtière for dinner, made by Mom's friend Maria, who lives down the road. After dinner I wrapped some gifts and went skating with Dad. Then he went off to the barn to talk to the sheep, as he does every Christmas Eve.

Now I'm lying in the bath. It's the first time in years I've had the urge to take a bath. It's steaming hot and I've added a few capfuls of some purple bubble stuff I found under the sink. It smells like purple bubbles should, lavender maybe.

I've actually been thinking about the song Mom's been

playing on repeat, "I'll Be Home for Christmas." I've decided the song is more about coming home for Christmas than just being home then. The implication that the singer has been away and is returning, that his stay will be temporary, makes the visit more meaningful. His presence is fleeting, so it must be cherished. It's different when you're already home for Christmas and will be remaining there when everyone else leaves.

A more appropriate song for me would be "I'll Be Staying for Christmas." You can plan on me. On Boxing Day I'll be walking down the driveway to open and close the gate. I'll trudge back to the house while everyone else drives away, their cars full of unwrapped gifts, to return to foreign countries, cities, to careers and stress, mortgage payments, ski weekends, fondue dinner parties, and children and commitments: the fervour of everyday life.

I must not have caught the latch in the door because Harry Snugs has joined me — in the room, not the bath. I was looking at the metal faucet between my feet when he slid in silently, pushing past the door and sidling up to stand at the rim of the tub on his back legs. His face is only a foot from mine. He examines me and meows.

I sink down a little lower in the tub. The foamy water inches up over my chin, mouth, and then ears. Only my nose, eyes, and forehead remain exposed. Tomorrow's Christmas morning. The turkey's defrosting in the fridge, all the gifts are under the tree, and everyone else is asleep. The skin on my hands is starting to prune.

I look around the bathroom. Harry Snugs is perched on the windowsill, his tail curled around his paws. With the water up over my ears, I'm deaf. The steaming water is a liquid barrier. It's the closest I've come to complete silence in weeks. All I can hear are odd vibrations in the water, my shifty leg brushing against the side of the tub.

The Christmas loaf is just out of the oven. It's packed with grains, fruit, nuts, and spices. I'm detaching some Christmas morning sleep from the corner of my eye as I watch Jimmy spread a soft knob of butter across a piece of the warm bread. It's melting as he spreads it. It's Jean's custom to make a fresh loaf first thing on Christmas morning, and Jimmy's arrived just in time to welcome it. He's brought some gifts and a couple of bottles of champagne with him. He's put the gifts under the tree, placed the bottles in the fridge, and cut himself a generous slice of warm bread.

Both orange and white cheddar and brie cheese have been opened and set on a wooden cutting board. Their plastic wraps are lying like snake skins on the counter. Someone's put muffins in a basket on the table and a jar of orange marmalade with a tiny spoon alongside it. Clementines are scattered across the counter like delicious juicy landmines. I can hear and smell the coffee brewing.

Three sips into my coffee, Jimmy hands me a flute of bubbling champagne. Drinking them together would be repulsive. Unpredictably, going back and forth is quite pleasant.

More guests arrive: Dad's sister, Aunt Grace; Mom's sister, Aunt Charlotte; her brother, Uncle Alec; and Grandma from Mom's side. They all live a short drive from the farm and they enter with food and parcels. Hugs are given and received. Someone suggests we should start opening gifts.

There's often an unintentional theme when it comes to the gifts. Last year a dozen or so candles were given and received. A few years back it was books. This year a lot of artisanal soap is exchanged. Uncle Alec wraps all his gifts in plastic grocery bags. I like it. It's his own style, and he's stuck with it over the years. I've stuck with tradition too, donning my frugal cap again this Christmas. I've made mix CDs for everyone.

"Don't forget," I remind the group endlessly as I hand out each one, "music lasts a lifetime."

"Even on these dodgy burned disks?" wonders Jimmy. "They aren't even in cases."

"They're still protected."

"You've just wrapped paper towels around them."

"Does anybody want more cheese?" I say.

Dad's the only one I don't burn a CD for. I pass him a card claiming I'll stop stealing his packs of chewing gum and razor cartridges. At the bottom I've written *Merry Christmas* in green and red pencil crayons.

We spend a few more hours opening gifts. The gift exchange would go by more quickly if it weren't for the five or six presents Mom and Dad give each other. They do the same thing every year, after promising not to give each other anything.

I'm sitting in between Dad and Mom. We've moved to the dinner table. The roasted turkey's in front of us; they always save our biggest one for Christmas. This year it's well over twenty pounds, probably closer to thirty. I have to avoid the lit candles to hand the china dish of lumpy mashed potatoes to Jimmy, who passes it along to Uncle Alec, who takes a dollop and hands it to Aunt Charlotte. Dad's helping Grandma with a spoonful of stuffing. Jean's more concerned with the baby than her meal, bouncing him on her knee and making faces. Johannes is pouring the wine, while Loa giggles at something that Jimmy has just said.

Mom lifts her glass in the air. "It's just so nice to have everyone here. It's been a great holiday." She takes a sip.

"Yes, it has," echoes Dad, raising his own. "Merry Christmas."

Everyone takes a drink. Then knives are scraping against plates and forkfuls of hot food are being brought up to mouths.

"And it's been so nice to see everyone again. You've all done such different things. That's what I can't get over," Grandma says.

Although Grandma has led her own adventurous and interesting life, it's always us, her grandchildren, that she wants to talk about. And we three are the only ones. Neither Charlotte nor Grace nor Alec has any children. We have no cousins. Other than Johannes, Loa, and George, it's been this same cast of characters sitting around the table at Christmas year after year.

We talk about some of Loa's exploits at school and how she's made the honour roll. Johannes, a history professor, has had an equally successful year, publishing a very popular non-fiction book that made the bestseller list in Iceland.

Grandma asks Jean if she's been back to any reunions at Oxford lately, which is where she completed her master's degree and met Johannes. Grandma's questions guide the river of conversation along Jean's path, from her days at Oxford to the ensuing years when she worked as the office manager of a graphic design company in England.

"It's better now that I'm my own boss," she says. Since arriving in Iceland Jean has become a busy freelance writer and editor.

And then the conversational river takes a bend when Aunt Grace navigates the discussion towards Jimmy. "How many people can say they've been involved in a shuttle launch?"

Jimmy's an engineer. He's been working for a company that's been hired by NASA and has been travelling back and forth to Florida or Texas whenever there's a shuttle launch.

"Not very many," says Alec.

"It's just a job," says Jimmy. "But, yeah, it's been good."

Now the current runs towards me. The table goes quiet as the discourse hits a dam. Mom takes another small sip of her wine. Some eyes fall upon me, others scan the table, looking to add more food to their crowded plates. Someone, I think Johannes, coughs. I'm pouring some extra gravy onto my mashed potatoes, forming a dark pool in the middle.

"Now," says Mom, "when was the last time you guys heard Iain whistle?"

"Not for ages," says Grandma.

"I'm not sure I've ever heard that," says Aunt Charlotte.

"Yes, I'd like that," affirms Grace.

"Oh, it's good stuff," answers Mom.

"Brilliant," declares Dad. "Come on, Iain, give them a little taste."

"Yes, we're all ears," says Jimmy.

My mouth is stuffed with turkey. I chew carefully and swallow without rushing. I wipe my mouth with my napkin, staining it with gravy, and put it down beside my plate in a ball. "Well, I mean, I wouldn't even know what to whistle."

"'Girl from Ipanema.'" Dad's prompt with his suggestion.

I stare at him in disbelief. "'Girl from Ipanema'?"

"Sure, everyone knows it."

"Right, then." I start in, gazing at the remains on my plate.

Grandma is swaying her head from side to side with the rhythm. Loa claps twice when I stop. Johannes and Jimmy exchange nods of approval. The baby seems poised to cry but resists. Uncle Alec asks Charlotte to pass the cranberry sauce while I retrieve my fork. The gravy on my plate is starting to congeal.

"Wait, what about something more festive now?" suggests Jean. She stands and walks away from the table with the baby in one arm.

"Absolutely," says Mom. "How 'bout 'I'll Be Home for Christmas'!"

"I don't know, I think one's enough for today," I say.

"Come on," says Dad, "one more."

No one else is as enthusiastic, or interested.

"Go on," says Mom, nodding towards Grandma, as if she's dying to hear it.

I acquiesce, puckering up and whistling until the plates around me are bare and we're ready for dessert. In the kitchen the baby starts to cry.

For the second time in as many days, I've temporarily removed myself from the world of sound. I thought it was impossible, but twice now I've deleted that sense. If I sit still there's no sound out here tonight. Nothing. Everything's frozen in place. It's rare not to be joined by a few of the animals by now. I haven't seen Titan or Meg or any of the cats. The sheep are locked up in the barn, and Lucius must be on a tree branch somewhere freezing his tail feathers off. When we finished dessert, I said I was just going out for a quick skate. I carried my skates outside, slung over one shoulder. But I haven't put them on yet. I didn't even turn on the floodlight. I'm just sitting in the dark, on the steep bank at the edge of the rink. I can see the activity in the house through the windows facing me.

Everyone is milling about. Dad's bent down, adjusting something on the stereo. Jimmy's feeling the effects of his meal, lying catatonic on the couch. Grandma's holding the baby. I've deduced over Christmas dinner that my three-month-old nephew, my thirteen-year-old step-niece, and even my elderly grandmother all have more active, rewarding social lives than I do. I bet Johannes has just cracked one of his racy European jokes, because everyone has started laughing.

A game has begun. I can't tell which. Another bottle of wine has been uncorked. They might be playing some form of charades or a trivia game. I know that teams have been picked, the way they are every year, by what colour paper crown each person found in their Christmas cracker. The crackers are pulled before we start eating, and everyone unfolds their crown and places it on their head. If your crown is red you'll be on the red team for the post-dinner games. I'm on the green team. Also on the green team are Jimmy and Grandma. They'll be competitive without me. Unlike me, Grandma is a charades ringer.

All the warm bodies and constant use of the oven have significantly raised the temperature in the house this week. No one really knows how cold it feels when it's only Mom, Dad, and me. But I was getting used to the cold.

I meant to bring my small silver flask outside with me. I topped it off with a few fingers of single malt, but feeling around in my coat pocket confirms that I've forgotten it. In its place I find my green crown. I unfold it and place it on top of my woollen toque. I look inside the house again. By the way people are wiggling about and bobbing their heads, I'd wager "Rockin' Around the Christmas Tree" just came on. I can see Uncle Alec snapping his fingers. I remove my mitt, reach down beside me, and close my bare fist around a ball of white snow. I bring it up to my mouth and take a bite. It's cold and wet.

The shape of my seat is hardening into the snowbank. I can feel it forming like drying cement underneath me. If it snows again, as they're calling for tonight, my imprint will be gone by morning. I'm not going to stay out here for long. I'll go back in and join my team. There's plenty of time, though. The games are just getting started.

Nine

Calendar Days

SINCE EARLY JANUARY I'VE BEEN wearing a lime green shawl over my shoulders whenever standing, lying, or sitting. It's my own dainty little way of preventing hypothermia. I swear, on the really cold days I can see my breath in the house. Mom and Dad tell me I'm being dramatic. They tell me to just wear more layers. Dramatic? I'm inside and that light fog floating around my face is my frozen breath.

Today I'm also wearing headphones. The music is too loud. It's distracting. The reason why I'm wearing them is to thwart the greater disturbance that's keeping me from writing. The sound is coming from the storage room, and it's been tormenting me since just after breakfast. Every few minutes the sound stops, and just as the tranquility settles in, it starts up again — on and off, all morning. I testily rip off the shawl, remove the headphones, and get up to investigate the noise.

I've been doing most things testily lately. My mood has soured along with the half-carton of eggnog lingering in the back of the fridge. It seems that slamming doors and yelling at the cats are my New Year's resolutions. I've also started growing an unkempt beard in the new year, for the hope of added warmth and because of my lack of disposable razor cartridges. Really, though, there's just no point shaving.

Do I even have to tell you how I spent my New Year's Eve? Seriously, just take a guess. Correct. I was at Lilac Hill with my parents. After our fondue supper we nursed weak gin-and-tonics while they sang several verses of "Auld Lang Syne." I tried twice, but Mom wouldn't let me go to bed until after midnight.

Since everyone left after Christmas, Mom, Dad, and I have been spending more time around each other. Mom's at the farm most days, and so is Dad. He's lecturing at the university only one day a week this term. He spends the majority of his time in his study. Mom is much less predictable, floating from room to room.

There's no holiday to look forward to anymore, just weeks of cold and snow. We have to shovel every couple of days and carry hay and buckets of water to the sheep, chickens, and ducks twice a day. The automatic watering system doesn't work in the winter, not at this farm anyway. When we're not bundled up, plodding through these daily outdoor tasks, we're all spending more time inside, around one another . . . bundled up.

I've probably set foot off our land only three or four times since Christmas. There's nowhere else for me to go, and I have little money to spend. Some days I feel that I should call CBC, hound them, plead for some more shifts. I haven't. Mostly I've been using my time to read, and I've been sleeping more, hibernating. In the afternoons, if I get some quiet, I write. So far the results have been mixed at best. I've produced some okay stuff and some horrible stuff.

I enter the storage room, muttering under my breath, and see Dad sitting with his back to the door. The room is a mess. He's surrounded by a moat of paper and is fiddling with something on the floor.

"Dad," I call over the grinding noise. "*Dad!*"

He flicks the switch on the machine and the room is suddenly quiet. He slowly turns his head. "You say something?"

"What's going on in here?" I'm holding my hands under each armpit, trying to keep them warm.

"Nothing," he says, removing a squished foam earplug from his right ear. "Just doing a bit of shredding."

I move closer to get a better view of Dad's equipment — a large grey shredding machine that looks worn and damaged. Beside it are several banker's boxes full of papers. He's seated on a footstool and his glasses are resting on top of his head. He places his hands on his hips and stretches his back.

"Since when do we have a shredder?"

"Since my mom died. I inherited it. I've been meaning to get it out for a while."

The protective plastic on the top of the shredder is dusty and cracked. Its black cord is flecked with white paint.

"How long did Grandma Reid have it for? I can't believe it still works."

"It's not that old; it works fine."

"Is it made to be so loud, though?"

"Meant."

"Pardon?"

"Is it *meant* to be so loud, and yes, you can't shred quietly. That would be an oxymoron."

I reach into the box and pull out a handful of papers.

"What are you shredding?"

"I'm cleaning out the filing cabinets."

I flip through the papers: old receipts, income tax forms, university newsletters.

"Dad, you're shredding old newsletters?"

"Among other things," he says.

The thin strips of red construction paper at the bottom of the shredder catch my eye.

"What other things?" I ask.

"Just documents and such. And there may have been some old valentines in there too."

"You're shredding our old valentines?"

"No, no. Just yours. There weren't very many of them. You can always pick them out and tape them back together if you really want to. I didn't put them in the fire."

The idea of taping those old paper hearts back together is deeply depressing, but for a moment I consider it. I pick out a few of the red strips. My name's spelled incorrectly on one of them, and it's signed by someone named Sam. I'm not a hundred percent certain, but I think Sam was the boy in my grade three class who was constantly being reprimanded for blowing his nose directly into the palm of his hand and rubbing the mucusy harvest onto his pants.

"No, no, it doesn't matter. Here, let me give you a hand."

Dad flips the switch back on and the shredder growls. I pick up the box, handing him one paper at a time. I watch him carefully feed each one through the sharp teeth of the machine. Our little assembly line continues to work in silence.

I've been noticing that Dad's arms and back are looking stronger, and the way he sits now, leaning in over the shredder, holding the paper out in front of him, accentuates his improved physique. Since cutting back on teaching he's had time to start going to the gym. I've never said anything but decide, now that we're alone, I should pass along some encouragement. It can't be easy going to the gym regularly, sitting in a cold car, driving through all that snow. I can't be bothered to do it and I'm not in my sixties. I'm not even thirty.

"You know, Dad, you're starting to look stronger; I can tell you've been lifting weights," I shout over the buzz.

He flicks off the machine. "I've been going for almost a year now. You know," he says, "you should think about coming with me. You could use a little exercise."

It's true. I could. My physical condition is nothing to be proud of. Like my disposition, it's taken a turn for the worse. While living in Toronto I walked every day, sometimes late at night. There are no streetlights here. Unlike me, the sun has better places to be these days, and it leaves each afternoon in a hurry. In Toronto they remove the snow from the sidewalks. Here the fields hoard the snow greedily and give it up only when the temperatures warm. Outside there's snow as far as the eye can see. I feel like I'm in the middle of an ocean — a white, frozen, boundless ocean.

It's the time of year when the charms of warm, meaty suppers and rocking chairs outweigh any benefits of working up a sweat or getting your heart rate going. Instead of going to the gym I've been meeting the roaring woodstove every morning and each night after supper; it's become pathological.

My last trip to the gym, a month or so prior, was with Mom. She convinced me that her yoga class would open up a whole new world to me. She claimed it would not only improve my limited flexibility and help me sleep better but also do wonders for my mood. She thought I seemed a little down in the dumps. When I insisted I'd never done yoga and had no intention of starting, she told me not to worry, that most of the women in the class were beginners too.

A week later I was removing my socks and unrolling a borrowed yoga mat in front of four retired women, three of whom were grandmothers. My mat was tattered and smelled of sweat. Everyone else seemed to have a new, clean mat. Mom's yoga for beginners didn't make me more nimble or elastic. Instead, from the first stretch I felt wooden and tense. After a brief warm-up we started with the basics. We were instructed to keep our legs straight, reach down, and touch our toes. I bent down as far as I could with unhinged knees, yet my toes remained far away. The backs of my legs ached. Our eyes were supposed to be closed, but I cheated, peering around the room with one eye. Everyone else was bent at the waist effortlessly, the tips of their fingers curled under their toes, inhaling and exhaling deeply. That was the first five minutes of class. It was a ninety-minute class.

In his quest for better health, Dad has turned to a row-ing machine and free weights. But with my yoga experience still fresh in mind, I'm reluctant to rush back to the gym. The time Dad works out isn't encouraging either. At least yoga class was at night. When Dad departs for the gym, I'm usually sound asleep under a dune of blankets.

"Well," I say, grabbing my elbow and stretching it across my chest, "I'd really like to, Dad, really, but I'm kinda busy the next few weeks with —"

"You're not busy," Dad's quick to say. "I was just checking the calendar this morning."

He's played his trump card. The calendar Dad refers to is a massive whiteboard mounted on the kitchen wall that displays a one-month period. At the end of each month the calendar is erased and the next month is created. Fresh-calendar day is always a big deal around the farm. The calendar is Dad's baby. He looks after it, keeps it clean. I notice him checking in on it several times a day, sometimes just standing a few feet away, sipping tea, looking at it affectionately. It's colour-coordinated, so all of Dad's engagements are marked in blue and Mom's schedule is in red. One evening I even found Mom adding to the calendar retroactively.

"That was last week; it doesn't need to go up there now," I pointed out.

"It's best just to put it up there." Her entry was a lunch date with three friends.

One night at supper, several weeks after I moved back home Dad presented me with my own dry-erase marker at an unofficial ceremony. "It's green," he said. "You're going to be green."

From then on I was constantly being reminded to add my plans, no matter how trivial, to the calendar. On the few occasions I actually had plans and remembered to mark them down, I forgot about my colour and would scribble my engagements in black. This would cause a flurry of confusion, and I would inevitably find my blunder corrected, switched to the proper green in Dad's hand.

So when Dad suggested I accompany him to the gym because I didn't have any plans, he wasn't assuming or guessing. He was relying on cold, hard fact. If the calendar says I'm free, I'm free.

"Do you think I can get in without a membership though?" I ask desperately. "I wouldn't want to ruffle any feathers."

"I've been saving up my guest passes. I could probably get you in for a year."

"Right," I say. "I guess it's a date then."

"I'll knock on your door tomorrow morning. But get your stuff ready tonight. I like to get there early."

And with that, Dad flips on the shredder, ending any further discussion. I retreat to my desk, slipping my shawl back onto my shoulders and wondering how I've just agreed to spend tomorrow morning doing sit-ups with Dad.

True to his word, Dad rips me from a deep sleep with a series of tenacious knocks on my door.

"You awake in there, bud? Time to go."

"Yup, just reading in here," I lie, squinting hatefully at the glowing display on my clock radio — 7:02 a.m. "I'll be right down."

Why didn't I go to bed earlier? I almost step on the empty beer glass and popcorn bowl sitting by my bed. Some-time around 1 a.m. I licked my finger and ran it around the bottom of the bowl and drained the last sip of beer. Now the bowl and glass get to stay in my warm room while I trudge down the hall to the bathroom. I feel betrayed.

Once downstairs, the scramble for my neglected gym clothes begins. I hadn't prepared the night before as instructed. As I frantically search for a clean shirt in the laundry basket by the door, I jump when I notice Mom sitting at the kitchen table in her dressing gown. I thought she was still sleeping. Her computer is on in front of her.

"What the hell's on your eye?" I ask.

Mom's wearing her usual morning attire for this time of year: several layers consisting of a sweater, sheepskin moccasins, and a housecoat with a fleece vest over top. All is status quo except for a damp brown lump she's wearing like an eye patch. Her head is tilted back slightly to keep the wad in place.

"Just a used teabag," she says, turning carefully. "Looks like another chilly morning out there. I should get the fire going."

"What's it doing on your eye?"

"Pumpkin got a little up close and personal last night." Mom's allergy to cats has dwindled over the years, but from time to time she still shows symptoms. Of all the cats, Pumpkin seems to bring out the worst of Mom's allergy. "Teabags are great for reducing swelling and soreness. It's the tannic acid."

"Noted," I say, hurriedly packing my old gym bag.

"Come and see this email I got this morning."

"I'm in a bit of a hurry, Mom."

"Seriously, check it out." She tilts the screen of her new computer in my direction. I scan her inbox. I only have to read the subject line to know I don't need to go any further. *The Amazing Walnut!*

"It lists all the ways walnuts are healthy. They are amazing."

Mom doesn't really look like a pirate, but because of her soggy eye patch I take a second to tell her she does anyway. I hear a honk from outside. Dad's waiting in his idling truck; grey exhaust is spiralling into the frigid air.

"I'm fine with that," Mom replies. "Better than a puffy-eyed boxer."

"I gotta go, Mom. Where's a clean towel?"

"Where they always are," she says. "Iain?"

"Yes," I say.

"What's a pirate's favourite restaurant?"

I don't have time for this. I lunge for my coat.

"I don't know, Mom."

She pauses. "Arrrby's."

"Good one, Mom. I seriously have to go . . . Dad's waiting . . ."

"But Iain . . ."

I freeze at the door. Looking back, I see a single brown tea tear dripping down Mom's cheek.

"Yes, Mom?"

"What's a pirate's favourite TV show?"

In the truck I can see Dad's frustration mounting on his face. He's looking in at the porch disconcertingly.

"Mom, I gotta go."

But before the door swings shut behind me, I hear her answer.

"*E-RRRRR!*"

At the gym Dad explains to the abnormally brawny fellow behind the desk that I'm his guest. I'm standing at his side, peeking over his shoulder as if I'm five. I want to stare at the floor and hold the cuff of Dad's jacket. Brawny Guy eyes me up and down, as if to say *You've got a lot of work to do.*

Dad, walking a couple of steps ahead of me, nods to everyone we pass. Most are hunched and limp along slowly; they all have white hair, if any at all.

In the change room I follow Dad to the lockers.

"I always use this one," he says, opening the metal door and kicking his shoes inside.

We're going to share a locker because I have no combination lock of my own. As Dad hangs his jacket to my left, a stranger flanks me to my right. He's older than Dad and has thinning grey hair. His wrinkled skin hangs loosely from his skeleton like a pink robe. His towel is draped over his shoulder and he's buck-naked. I'm sitting on the wooden bench staring at the empty locker straight ahead. The old naked man turns towards Dad and rests his left foot on the bench. "This damn cold is here to stay," he says, laying his towel on the ground. "That wind feels ruthless."

That's because you're naked, I want to remind him.

"Yup, it's pretty cold," says Dad indifferently. "Nothing we can do about that."

The old man takes a comb from the top shelf of his locker and begins to slick back his damp hair. As he grooms himself, a second naked man of a similar vintage appears, popping out from behind the neighbouring bank of lockers.

"Done your exercise for another day?" he asks the first old naked man.

"You bet," he answers. "This is my favourite time of day."

The two stand casually together, continuing their discourse as I lace up my running shoes.

Loafing along on the treadmill, I'm watching a woman in front of me doing chin-ups. As she reaches up to grab the silver bar for another set, the front edge of her tight shirt comes up slightly. For a second I catch a glimpse of her stomach. I can see her ribs pressing against her skin, and it reminds me of the skeletal frame of the unfinished barn in one of the neighbouring fields when I was growing up.

I look to my left and my right. When did this fitness revolution take place? When did this running, stepping, and gliding on electronic machines in front of TVs become the accepted form of exercise, replacing morning walks and working outdoors?

To be fair, some aren't watching TV; some are reading trashy celebrity gossip magazines. Aren't most of the photos airbrushed and modified on computers? I guess virtue has become linked to our appearance. To be moral is to be in shape. The Greeks had their omniscient gods built on myths and we have ours.

As I walk along on the treadmill, I spot the muscular guy from the front counter sweeping up what appears to be a small mound of mud. He looks irked. I follow the mud droppings from the change-room hall to the water fountain to the treadmill I'm walking on, and then to my shoes. I forgot that I've been wearing these same running shoes — my only pair — in the barn. I could go and change into the shoes I wore to the gym, but they're heavy winter boots. Not an option. I have to stick with my muddy runners, even if the dirt is laced with sheep manure. I'm aware that I'm not making any friends.

When the digital readout on the treadmill indicates I've been walking for eleven minutes, two women with chunky legs squeezed into tight black pants start arguing about whose turn it is next. The entire row of treadmills is occupied. The woman who's been walking beside me explains that she has only five minutes of her workout left. The other woman is holding a clipboard, passive-aggressively claiming that it doesn't matter because she's signed up for the machine now.

Eleven minutes should be good for me. I'm sweating. The guy with the broom is getting closer anyway, and the women seem upset that there's new competition for their machines. I hit the Stop button, spray down the machine, smile at the ladies in tight pants, and head for the weights.

"Lookin' to workin'?" a man asks, hopping up and down on the spot. He's the closest thing to my peer. I'd put him somewhere in his early fifties but he looks to be in reasonable shape. He's wearing a tank top and a baseball hat and has a trimmed salt-and-pepper goatee. As I walk over, he's between sets.

"Sure," I say. "My legs could use some work." *My legs could use some work?*

"Lemme just get one more set in first."

Without waiting for a response, he steps back to the

equipment, focuses somewhere in front of him, and begins his set. The machine has two black handles suspended just above the floor. The user is meant to bend at the knees, grab the handles, stand, and then bend again, all the while maintaining a straight back. The exercise is called a dead lift. It's meant to strengthen the legs and lower back. As soon as he starts, the man's formerly amiable face twists into a tight red mass of veins. With each lift he releases a deep, glottal moan. The harder the set becomes, the louder he grunts and the more he contorts his face. On his final rep he releases what can only be described bluntly as a wail, which lasts for several seconds. I look around the gym, expecting a reaction, but no one seems to notice. He releases the handles, rolls his shoulders, and looks at me.

"Okay, you ready?" he asks.

I nod and move into position, gripping the warm handles. Just as I'm poised to begin, he starts tapping my muddy left shoe with his pristine white one.

"You need to be a little wider," he's saying. "Just a little." I silently obey, moving my foot a few inches to the left. "No, too far," he snaps. "Just keep 'em shoulder width. Shoulder width is key."

We continue this dance — a little wider, a little closer — until he backs away, bobbing his head in satisfaction. "Perfect," he says. "Now you're ready."

Keeping my feet planted in exactly the same position proves tricky. By rep five my legs are starting to tremble. By seven I can barely make it back up again. By eight I'm done. An underwhelming first set by any standard.

When the man in the cap takes the handles again, I'm curious to see how long he takes to set his own feet after spending what felt like several hours on mine. But he begins instantly. His feet are at least a foot outside shoulder width. It's not even close. When he finishes, I'm waiting for some explanation as to why his feet were so wide apart, but he says nothing and again motions for me to take over.

"Don't forget," he says, tapping me on the shoulder and heading for the water fountain, "shoulder width and you'll be fine."

I remove half of the weights and perform my second and final set. The dead lifts have tired me out. I grab a soft blue mat from a pile and head for an isolated corner. I complete one set of twenty push-ups, fleetingly consider doing the same number of sit-ups, and opt instead to flop down on my back.

I lie there for a long time, breathing through my nose and staring up at the ceiling. I flip over onto my stomach and watch all the elderly jocks. I'm struck by the irony of their morning workouts. Mostly they stand in groups of three or four, talking and joking, occasionally shuffling over to a machine to pull some type of weighted cable. Others sit, bouncing on large colourful rubber balls. If they were fifty or sixty years younger and wearing snowsuits, I'd swear they had just been plucked from recess. Their lack of strenuous activity makes me feel better about my own unproductive morning.

Towelling off in the locker room, I turn to Dad. He's sitting on the bench beside me, red-faced and shirtless.

"How was the workout, Dad? You must have been rowing for a good thirty-five minutes."

"Not great," he says. "I lost something."

"What do you mean?"

"Look," he says, holding up his earphones. "Something's missing." I take the earphones from Dad. One of the protective foam pieces is absent. "It must have fallen off during my workout. I have no idea how it could have happened."

Dad is noticeably dejected. It's an unfortunate end to our maiden workout, but I can't seem to find the appropriate words of condolence. So instead we both pull on our clean socks in silence.

On the way home we stop for refreshment. We sit in the truck in our parkas and toques, listening to the classical music station, sipping hot coffee and chatting intermittently.

"I bet you'll be sore tomorrow," he says. "And the next day after, it'll be even worse."

"Probably," I answer, looking out the foggy window. "But if I'm really sore, maybe I can borrow some used teabags from Mom."

"Pardon?" asks Dad.

"Nothing."

As we pull out of the parking lot, Dad abruptly moves his hand up to his ear. "Well, that's amazing. Look at this," he says, eagerly. "It must have been in there the whole time."

I look for only a second. I'm not sure if it's the foam piece from his headphones he's holding between his fingers or one of his shredding earplugs. I decide to leave it a mystery. As we drive home I can't help but wonder when I'll be losing my own belongings in my ears.

It may not be tomorrow, but soon Dad will suggest that I use another of his guest passes. He'll tell me I won't be so sore the next time, that it's good for me, and that I'll start to see a difference soon. He'll tell me the morning exercise routine will start to feel habitual, and if I stick to it those buckets of water won't feel so heavy.

It's late now. I wander into the kitchen and turn on the light. I stand hunched in front of the calendar, searching for any hint of green. Green is the colour of hope, but the board is a disheartening mess of blue and red. According to Dad's colour-code system, I don't exist. In the eyes of the calendar, I'm invisible.

I can feel my calf muscles and hamstrings tightening up. I should probably eat a banana or something. Dad's next planned gym visit is seared in blue, only two days away. I reach out and pick up my green marker. I uncap it and give the soft tip a sniff. It smells new and looks wet. I move it up to the calendar, but I have nothing to add.

Ten

Lost In Winter

It's the second week of February. The wind is harsh, more consistent and less lenient than in the city. It never felt this unbearable when I was young. I'm much less durable now. If I carry water out to the sheep or table scraps to the chickens, the cold can actually help me along, sharpen my conviction. But if I'm outside without resolve, the cold will pull me even further away from it. I feel smaller, more delicate. If you tried to convince me the whole world is frozen today, covered in snow and ice, I might believe you. I think it is. The world is frozen. It is.

I'm standing still with my chin burrowed into my chest. This wind has rendered my cotton pants useless. They're as protective as tissue paper, and are beginning to take on the same texture. My old rubber boots are equally defenceless. My feet have hardened into two unserviceable mounds. I blow into my gloved hands, more a symbolic gesture than a practical one.

I've been summoned outside by Dad. I was still in the

bathroom when I heard him calling. It was just after 7:30 a.m. "Iain, I need you outside," he called from the door. "ASAP."

I spat out a mouthful of toothpaste and watched the white saliva escape down the drain before going downstairs. I've been taking a more active role with the outdoor chores. Since I'm still at the farm and haven't been working, I thought helping more with the animals would be both suitable and fair. So these days it's not uncommon for me to be outside early in the morning giving Dad a hand. But his voice was different this morning, his call more emphatic.

I grabbed a banana for breakfast. I've been having trouble with fruit. My banana wasn't normal — it was too sweet. It was definitely sweeter than any other banana I've ever had; it tasted like someone had sprinkled sugar on it and closed it again. I didn't hate it, but it wasn't good. And yesterday I peeled an orange and found a single white hair inside. Explain that to me. I've decided I'm off fruit. My body will have to make do.

I chewed the sweet banana, yanked my scarf up high around my neck, and pulled my hat down low on my head. I found Dad, holding a shepherd's crook, standing beside the poultry pen. He brought some of his students out to help build it when we first moved to the farm. It's whitewashed and has a slanted shingled roof and a small opening like a dog door cut into the side. This morning the shingles are wearing silver frost like a coat of paint. Sharp icicles hang over the roof's edge like fangs.

Dad looks crestfallen, like he's just found a hair in his orange. His breath is hanging in the air around him. He tells me we've lost a duck, the pretty one with the brown feathers. I look around. There's no sign of a predator or intruder, no marks of a struggle, no blood-streaked snow or feathers frozen into the ground. Just five ducks quacking impatiently inside the wire fence, waiting for their bits of stale bread, instead of six.

"We better look for her," he says.

We turn into a two-man search party, stumbling around the outside perimeter of the coop. For a moment I'm distracted by the sight of Dad's magnolia tree, the one he planted last summer. I stop in my tracks. I can't see the actual tree, only its hidden form, which is covered in a heavy blanket of snow. It's a morbid scene. I can't believe it'll be alive come spring. There's no way. Not after all the snow we've had this year.

I don't say anything to Dad; he's busy searching for the duck. I start moving again along my unformed path, the cold stinging my cheeks. Neither of us is a proper farmer, which is confirmed during times like these. The snow is oppressively high, reaching up over our knees.

"Come here, girl. Come on now, where are ya?" I'm calling. I hear myself making exaggerated kissy noises.

When one of the dogs goes missing, usually the requisite name-calling will bring it bounding back. Just the possibility of some attention sends their tails wagging uncontrollably. And if you have trouble finding one of the cats, just shake a bag of salmon-flavoured treats. Within seconds they will descend upon you, circling your feet, rubbing their heads affectionately against your shin like furry beggars.

I've learned that ducks are a different sort. Ducks are hard to track. They can't be cajoled, they don't have proper names to call, and they aren't interested in long belly rubs. Ducks are cautious by nature and skeptical of your motives. When approached, their tendency is to huddle together like a football team and then waddle or, worse, fly away. If they take to the air you're in trouble. My kissing sounds are growing louder, more elaborate. I hear myself clicking, whistling; eventually I'm making a noise that resembles yodelling. It won't do any good but it can't hurt.

"You better stop all that," Dad calls from the other side of the pen. "If she's still around you'll just scare her away with all that fussing."

When our paths converge, neither of us is optimistic. I shrug my shoulders, Dad shakes his head. "There's no sign of her, not with all this blowing snow."

We watch the remaining ducks cluster together in the middle of the pond. Ice has covered it like everything else in our vicinity, but the ducks still feel safer there. They're quacking suspiciously, ardently, as if something is wrong.

Our search party reconvenes inside with a pot of coffee by the crackling fire. We're joined by Mom. She stands behind Dad's armchair in her housecoat and pyjamas. Dad and I remove our jackets and gloves but leave on our toques. Our faces are red and numb. We lean in towards the fire. I hold my warm mug in both hands. The hot coffee is divine.

"What do you think happened?" asks Mom. "Doesn't look like a wolf or a fox."

"Probably neither," says Dad, without looking up from the fire.

We talk intermittently; every so often a suggestion is put forth. Some ideas are cast aside, others seem more likely. We conclude that the drifting snow packed up against the fence must have acted as a ramp, an easy exit from the enclosure. That's as far as we get until Dad slides his hat off and lays it across his thigh. He scratches his head. "You know what? I bet it's the wind."

"I was thinking that too," agrees Mom. "Once she got out, she probably just blew away. The wind has been so strong the last couple of days. It always is in February."

"And it was howling again last night."

"Wait — you think a duck, an animal with the ability to fly, just blew away in the wind?"

"Yes," they answer together.

"She was oldest of the group and definitely the smallest," says Dad, staring at the orange coals. "With the wind and all the snow she would have been completely disoriented."

I can't believe a duck could blow away like an empty plastic bag, but I don't press the issue. Dad sips his coffee without talking. Mom brings one hand up over her mouth; with the other she pats Dad softly on the back. She doesn't hold her hand there long, but still I notice.

At lunch Dad's still visibly distressed. He's swirling his spoon around in his soup. I think it's more than just the duck that's troubling him. It's the time of year. The cold and snow are harsher than they used to be. It seems to take Dad longer to get dressed for the morning chores, and the water pails and feed bags seem a little heavier. It's understandable:

he's been carrying them for almost thirty years. He tells me unenthusiastically that he's got to pick up a load of hay after lunch. I tell him I have nothing on, so I'll tag along and help him load it up.

As I watch Dad finish his soup, I see a familiarity in his hands. I've never noticed it before. His hands are slightly larger, but they are my hands. And my hands are his.

As I write my name in the snow, it's hard to deny the uncharacteristic quality of the cursive lettering. The stylish loops and precise symmetry easily trump my regular penmanship. Dad and I have stopped on the way home from our hay run. The back of the truck is loaded with fifteen bales. Two minutes ago I looked at Dad and said, "Sorry, I have to pee."

"Me too," he answered. "Must be all that coffee."

We pulled onto a side road that we've passed hundreds of times but have never explored. About a hundred yards in the road curves to the left and then twists steeply uphill. It levels out again above the highway. The view is wonderful. We can see out over the rolling white fields for miles.

"Hey," Dad calls over his shoulder, "what a view from up here. It's lovely."

I walk over to the front of the truck and lean against the hood. Dad joins me. "I hope you don't have to go anywhere tonight. They're calling for some heavy snow again. Driving won't be very nice."

"I'll be around," I say.

"The hockey game's on TV; you want to watch it?" he asks.

"Maybe, yeah."

For a while we stand quietly in the cold and admire the unexpected view.

The next morning we get a phone call from our neighbours across the road. They're in possession of a small duck with brown feathers. Maybe it belongs to us? They thought at first it was a wild duck, but when they approached her, opening the front door of a cat cage, the duck happily waddled in and waited patiently for them to close it. Knowing we had a small flock, they called us. We were thrilled, Dad especially. The duck's return has given him a boost.

Still, I'm surprised when he stops me in the hall, wondering if I have an extra tennis ball lying around. To my knowledge, Dad's never played tennis. Neither have I.

"But I've seen you dribbling one around the house before."

"Maybe a rubber ball, but I haven't seen a tennis ball around here since high school."

"Well, there has to be one around somewhere."

I find one buried in the back of the front hall closet. It's wedged into the toe of a muddy hiking boot. The felt is completely worn off, the rubber creased and exposed. Meg's crater-like teeth marks are embedded in its surface.

Dad is pleased. "I knew we had one lying around."

"You can't use it though, Dad. Look, it's an old chew toy." I toss it to him.

He catches it with both hands, basket-style. "Perfect." He takes the ball and withdraws to his study.

Twenty minutes later I walk past Dad's study while talking on the phone to my pal Sheldon. The door's open, and I stop and turn around. I pop my head in and see Dad leaning against the wall beside his bookcases. He's standing like a statue, keeping his back straight; he slowly lowers down into a sitting position before standing again. He does it over and over. His eyes are closed.

Sheldon's still talking to me. "You seem different today. You sound unusually happy."

"Course, man — we got our duck back! It blew away the other day, and we had no idea what happened or where it went or if it was even still alive or anything, and anyway, our neighbours called this morning and it turns out they found it in their yard. They thought it was wild, but it wasn't. It was our duck, and she's the smallest one and she's really pretty. Unreal, eh?"

Sheldon breathes in and out a couple of times. "It's a duck you're talking about?"

"Yeah."

"You have others, right?"

"We do, yeah."

"I mean, I guess it's pretty cool."

Sheldon changes the subject, asking if I've been getting any shifts at CBC these days. I tell him I haven't. I tell him that instead I've been helping out with the chores, and that I've also been writing more. I've been trying my hand at some humorous stuff. I ask if he wants to hear any. He agrees. When I finish reading, there's no reaction. Then he says, "Yeah, that's funny, man. Nice."

Here's the thing: if something actually is funny, people

don't say so. They laugh. Saying something's funny but not laughing is just fraudulent.

"Funny stuff," he says again.

Sheldon wonders what my plans are for the weekend. I tell him I don't really have any. I'll probably just hang around Lilac Hill. I tell him he's welcome to come by if he wants, but he can't. He's going to visit his parents for the weekend. He tells me he hasn't seen them in a few months. They live only about an hour away but Sheldon tells me he's had a busy few months with work. Sheldon's some type of accountant.

"Yeah, we'll probably watch the hockey game or something. I find the older he gets, the harder it is to relate."

"Yeah, totally." I'm watching Dad. He's still squatting up and down. I notice the old tennis ball rolling along the wall behind him like a ball bearing. "I know what you mean."

When I get off the phone, Dad's finished his unconventional exercise. He looks more relaxed. He's waiting for me, holding out the ball. "This will work wonders on your back."

"What?"

"It's a special exercise, meant to relax the muscles of your back."

"How do you know I have a sore back?"

"Because I do."

"So, you're in your sixties. I'm not even thirty yet. Your back is always sore."

"Just give it a try."

I oblige without objection. Yesterday's walk through the snow with the hay bales has done a number on me.

I take the ball and hold it between the wall and my spine. I start squatting up and down.

"Am I right? How does that feel? Pretty good, eh?"

"Yeah," I say, "it feels better already."

Dad stays where he is, observing the process with a grin.

If my back were the only thing ailing me, I wouldn't have bothered making an appointment. I can cope with a stiff lower back. But that's not all. I've developed several complaints this winter. They're getting worse, and since it's been years since my last physical, I decide now is a good time to see my doctor again.

Initially I wanted to get a full physical, the standard once-over. But when I called, the nurse said I would have to book it a couple of months in advance. So I just said I wanted to see him about my eyes. "They're bugging me," I said.

I'm sitting on a padded table with a sheet of white paper spread across the top. My feet are dangling over the side. Whenever I shift or raise one buttock, the paper crinkles. It's an antiseptic, lonely room. There are laminated placards on the wall detailing certain areas of the human body; others outline the benefits of vitamin D supplements and hand-washing. A stack of Kleenex boxes and two glass containers are sitting on the counter beside the sink; one jar holds cotton balls, the other tongue depressors. I hate tongue depressors.

The doctor enters, closing the door behind him. We say hello and share a few affable minutes talking about the cold weather and hockey. He asks me how things are going and what I've been up to. What have I been up to? I've gone days without writing an original word and have had nothing to occupy me but time and routine. One of my preferred methods of dealing with this slump has been to think of lengthy palindromes and print them on a blank sheet of paper. I read the words over and over in my head. For some inexplicable reason these phrases ease my frustration. If I were honest I would say, *Able was I ere I saw Elba.*

"Just keeping busy," I say.

Then the doctor sits on his little stool and wheels closer. "So, what's been bothering you?" he asks.

"It's my eyes."

"How so?"

"I'm not sure exactly. They seem to be more sensitive to light, and sometimes they're bloodshot. They never used to be bloodshot. And whenever I look at something white, like a field of snow or a blank computer screen, I can see black dots." He shines a small handheld light into each of my eyes and writes something on my chart. "It's almost like someone has come along and put a few dots on my cornea with a black Magic Marker."

"It's nothing to worry about," he says evenly. "And there's nothing you can really do about it. They're just floaters, and they're quite common, although it's rarely seen in someone your age. It mostly happens when people get older and the gelatin at the back of the eye starts to disintegrate."

"Oh."

"Are you feeling healthy aside from your eyes?"

"I think so. Well, mostly. I find that I, well, I find that I go to the bathroom more than anyone I know. Like, pee, I mean. I pee more than anyone. Even more than old people. Maybe

I'm drinking too much coffee. I've been drinking a lot."

It's true. I've become an addict. I even find pleasure in the discreet gurgle and steamy hiss of percolating coffee. I love opening the bag of imported beans and plunging the lower half of my face into the skinny black packet before sprinkling the inky beans into the grinder and watching as they whirl into a fine powder. Hearing the hot water trickling through the ground beans while anticipating the aromatic offspring is my daily fascination. Seriously, I look forward to this process more than anything.

I'm reminded of the literary critic John Bayley, who noted, "Routine needs a change, and change finds some relief again in routine, like the people in Dante's hell who kept being hustled from fire into ice bucket, then back again ... Routine has no suggestions to make." So it's coffee that has become the anchor of my daily routine. Coffee has the amazing ability to change people, not fundamentally or recklessly like certain drugs, but by modestly nudging their mood into a warmer, more cognizant, more alert, and, most important, more confident direction. I've even pinned up above my desk the most recent palindrome I wrote: *Lived on decaf, faced no devil.*

"Again," he says, "I don't think that's anything serious or anything you can treat or should be concerned about. It's just your physical makeup. Have you always been that way?"

I'd forgotten one of my more endearing childhood nicknames until right now: Peein' Iain.

"Yeah, I guess I have."

"Nothing to worry about, then."

"Well then, the only other thing is my wrists and ankles. I've been experiencing some pain after shovelling snow and carrying hay."

"If I remember, you've had some history with bone chips, right?"

"Yeah, I've had a couple."

He takes my left wrist in his hand and taps on either side with his index finger. "That's something you'll have to watch. Your mom has osteoporosis, doesn't she?"

"Yeah, she does. But she never seems to complain about pain in her joints."

"Well, you should probably start getting your bone density checked. It's hereditary. And make sure you're getting enough calcium."

When we finish the consultation, the doctor follows me out into the hall. We instantly switch into acquaintances mode and away from doctor–patient mode. We don't chat as though I've just confided in him the details of my overactive bladder, but rather as if we've just bumped into each other at the mall.

"Good to see you, Iain," he says, shaking my hand. "Say hi to your parents."

"Will do."

Driving home, I'm questioning my decision to visit the doctor. I like him. He's a very good, thorough doctor, but my back is still stiff. I realize we didn't even talk about my back; I forgot to mention it. I feel the same as I did driving there. That's not true. I feel worse. It's been confirmed that I have the eyes and bladder of a seventy-year-old man and the bone density of an eighty-year-old woman.

Back at Lilac Hill I find Mom lying on her heating pad on the couch. It's a sure sign her back is sore.

"Is your back sore now too?"

"It's not a big deal. It's just a little stiff."

"What happened?" I'm standing only a foot or two away from the fire, warming my backside, wishing I could just sit down right on top of the stove.

"I hung a few of your Dad's shirts on the shower rack upstairs, 'cause I like to not use the dryer whenever possible, and you know how heavy your Dad's big shirts are when they're wet."

"No, not really."

"Well, they're very heavy, and the next thing I know the whole shower curtain has fallen down. So I tried to put it back up and I must have tweaked my back."

"Why didn't you call Dad to help?"

"I would have, but *his* back is sore right now, and I thought if I asked for his help he might hurt it even more."

She thought the shirts were too heavy for Dad to lift up without hurting his back, so she did it? I bow my head and close my eyes instead of trying to explain to Mom how preposterous her logic is. I hear Dad's study door creak open. He joins us in the living room.

"How's your back?" he asks Mom. "Any better?"

"Yeah, a bit better, I think."

"I wish you had just called me," he says.

"What about you? How's your back feeling?"

"I would say better."

"Better's good," says Mom.

"Yes."

"How much better?" she asks.

"Not *better* better," replies Dad, "but better."

"Like mine," says Mom. "Just better."

"Yup, better, but not all better."

I can't take it. "Butter," I say.

"What?"

"Nothing," I mumble as I stagger upstairs to bed.

My brother Jimmy joins us for Sunday dinner. We haven't seen much of him since Christmas. He's been busy with work. He's just returned from a trip to Australia, where the weather was hovering around thirty degrees Celsius. He looks good, tanned and fit.

Apart from the cutlery scraping along the plates, the table's quiet. I tell Jimmy about my sweet banana. And about my hairy orange. He's unmoved. I tell him about the duck. We debate whether the duck flew away or blew away. I want him to see how the lack of impetus, the lack of choice on the duck's part, makes the story much sadder. But Jimmy's showing only slightly more interest in the story than Sheldon. He wonders what else has been going on around the farm.

"Our backs have been sore," says Dad.

"All of us," adds Mom. "Tight and sore."

Jimmy is busy cutting through pieces of baked trout with the edge of his fork.

"You know, I had this same cheese today at lunch," Dad says, holding up a piece of broccoli with melted cheese. I'm not sure if it's also a response to my brother's question or simply a general declaration.

I put my fork down and jump in. "No, no. Mom makes your cheese buns with the old cheddar when you lecture on Tuesdays. She uses the processed cheese for grilled cheese."

Dad looks at me ponderously and nods. I look over at Jimmy; he too sets his fork down.

"How do you know what cheese Dad eats?"

A great question; how do I know that? "Well —"

"You know what? It doesn't really matter." He picks up his fork in his tanned hand and continues eating.

After dinner Mom's circling the table, retrieving and stacking empty dishes. My brother has gone home with the leftovers. He's scheduled to be in Florida in a week.

I haven't moved from the table. Dad's watching TV upstairs and I'm asking Mom how she's feeling these days. I'm wondering if the winters are getting harder for her too.

"I feel a little tired, I guess. It's just age."

"What about Dad?"

"He's feeling good. Although I think you're right — winter is getting a little harder for him."

"I think they might be getting harder for me too."

"Well, it's always around each new decade you feel changes," she says. "Fifty, sixty, seventy. Your dad and I felt it when we hit sixty, and I think your grandma felt it at ninety. That's why she bought her new car last year in the winter. Buying the new hybrid just gave her an extra boost."

"What about thirty?"

"Well," Mom replies, "thirty's possible."

"Isn't that too early for a dramatic change?"

"You never know. Age affects everyone at different times of their lives. Everyone gets older at a different pace."

"I guess."

She puts the stack of dirty plates back down on the table and sits in her chair. "So, have you been doing much writing lately?" she asks.

"A bit," I say. I want to explain how I know I should be doing more. How without the constraints of a day job I have the time here at the farm. I want to make the comparison to basketball and how a wide-open shot, when you have all the time you need to set yourself up and shoot without rushing, is often a more difficult shot to make than just catching and shooting in rhythm, without thinking about it, even if someone's pressuring you. I have the time to write but it's still a struggle, and the results are suspect. Some days are better than others, and there's nothing else I'd rather be doing, but I feel like I've been missing a lot of open shots.

"Well, there's nothing you can do," she says. "If you're a writer, you're a writer. It's a calling."

"I suppose."

"No point in trying to fight the inevitable," she says, as she clears my plate.

I stay at the table for a few minutes, gaping at the wall. Mom's humming in the kitchen as she washes up and puts food away. I'm wondering exactly what I have to show for the past couple of months when I hear Dad call me from upstairs. "Iain, I think you might enjoy this."

I find Dad seated in his armchair. "I've seen this one before," he says, "but it's quite interesting: a biography of Shakespeare that focuses mainly on his love sonnets.

I imagine they're airing it now for Valentine's Day."

I collapse onto the couch, grabbing the heavy wool blanket from the back. Within a minute my eyes are slipping shut. Dad nudges me softly on the arm. I cough, blink a couple of times, and stretch out my legs so far off the end of the couch that my slippers fall off. I blink again. Dad raises the volume of the TV a couple of notches. He levers out the footrest of his blue La-Z-Boy. I look around the room. The curtains aren't shut tight, and the outdoor sentinel light, reflecting off the snow on the roof, is beaming in through the two-inch gap. A pale yellow path runs from the window along the middle of the floor to me and Dad. I can hear the wind rattling against the glass.

"You shouldn't nap now, bud," he says. "You'll never sleep tonight."

Spring

Eleven

Back to School

I'M STANDING AT MY CLOSET, holding a white button-up, collared shirt in my left hand. In my right I'm holding a faded blue T-shirt with the bearded face of Ernest Hemingway printed on the front. There are decisions to be made. Tomorrow, for the first time in years, I'm going back to school. Not to sit in on a university lecture or speak to a high school class, but to elementary school, where it all started, to revisit grade one.

My aunt Grace is a primary school teacher. This year she claims that obedience, respect, and fun radiate from her students. She calls it her dream class. Since I'm back at Lilac Hill, she insists I take part in something called Visitor's Day, a morning when a guest comes in to help with the kids' activities. Grace has been telling me for months that spending some time away from the farm and around kids will do me some good.

I drop the white shirt back down on the shelf in a wrinkled heap. I'm going with Hemingway for practical reasons.

If, as I fear, I'm a disappointment to the kids and have nothing to say, Ernest will be more of a conversation starter than a tedious shirt and tie. *So, kids, what did you guys think of* The Old Man and the Sea? *Maybe a touch too theistic?*

Anything but a wooden barrel held up with wide suspenders will be an improvement over my recent attire. I've been taking advantage of the lax dress code at the farm by wearing an old pair of sweatpants I found in my closet. I love them and have been wearing them every day. The benefits of an elastic waistband are many. No pockets? No problem. What do I need pockets for at the farm?

Before bed I rummage through my room, trying to find an old picture of myself from grade one. I can't even remember what a kid in grade one looks like. I know they're short, and that's about it. I'm able to unearth a picture of myself when I must have been around twelve. I'm sitting on the couch playing a black clarinet with a songbook open in front of me. I haven't seen the picture in years. There's a glowing red pimple in the middle of my forehead that looks like a large, misplaced nipple. One of my eyes is closed, the other is squinty. I'm wearing green silky pyjama bottoms, no shirt, and a worn fedora. I decide that this image is the purest and deepest representation of awkwardness. I fold it twice and throw it under my bed.

I fall asleep fully clothed, delighting some more in my sweatpanted legs, and hoping the six-year-olds will be much more graceful and refined than my twelve-year-old self. Or my twenty-seven-year-old self, for that matter.

I've hit the perfect water temperature this morning, a rare feat. Plus the hot water is lasting for longer than usual. Ironically, in these conditions it seems wasteful to have a short shower. So I linger. I feel as if I could stand under the warm jet of water until summer.

In the kitchen Mom offers to make me breakfast. "Just like your first day of grade one," she alleges. "I think I made you some fried eggs then too."

When she places the plate of steaming eggs and toast in front of me, I see a patch of dry, red skin near her temple. It looks sore and itchy.

"Whoa, what happened there? Did something bite you?'

"What do you mean?"

"That rash."

"Oh, that, yeah. No, no, nothing bit me. I'm just allergic to the cellphone. That's why I rarely use it. And when I do, I have to remember to hold it an inch or so away from my face."

I dunk my first piece of toast into one of the yolks. "Sorry, Mom, for a second there I thought you said you were allergic to the cellphone."

"I did." She sits down now, tucking into her own plate of hot breakfast.

I rub my forehead with my hands. If I wasn't feeling so anxious about my class visit I might ask Mom to expound on her peculiar cellphone allergy. As it is, I don't. I strongly consider just standing up, bowing once, and heading back to the shower. Instead I finish my eggs and clear my plate.

Outside I'm not surprised to find my windshield in need of a scrape. As usual, spring is late for her own party.

I'm running late too, and when I can't find a scraper, I resort to using a small bottle of hand sanitizer I keep in the glove compartment to grind off the frozen condensation on the glass. It takes much longer than it should and fundamentally reinforces why I live with my parents and have no job. I can't help imagine what my grade one teacher would think if she saw me now.

Luckily I'm able to find the red-brick school, which is tucked inside a new residential development, without much difficulty. Children in boots and winter jackets are walking in groups of three and four along the sidewalk. They're my compass. I pull into one of the last remaining parking spots and head inside.

I catch a glimpse of myself in the glass of the front door. It's a dreary sight. My blossoming beard, untrimmed in weeks, is a shaggy, homely mess. The circles under my eyes look darker than usual. I look like I've just rolled out of a bed made from a flattened cardboard box in a bus shelter. I hope I don't frighten the children.

In the main office a friendly lady with curly grey hair gives me a name tag and directs me to the staff room. There's a pot of coffee brewing on the counter that I smell before I see. Most teachers have already made their way to class; a handful are delaying the inevitable. Grace introduces me to the remaining few. I shake some hands and offer the requisite small talk.

"So you're just here of your own accord?" a sociable teacher with dangling apple earrings asks. "That's brave."

"Yup, just thought it would be a fun change of pace."

"And you had no problem getting off work for the morning?"

"I was persistent."

"Well, send him to my classroom when he's done," she says to Grace. "If he hasn't already run back to his car screaming."

Grace and the lady share a lengthy chuckle. I yawn, scratch my beard, and stare longingly at the brewing coffee. I stopped for a cup on my way but would love a second. I wonder if the entire pot is already spoken for. Surely there aren't enough teachers left to drink a whole pot?

"He's really great." I turn around to see a man dressed in a black turtleneck sweater and green khakis. He looks to be only a few years older than me, but he's at least a foot shorter (his eyes are at my armpit). His hands are in his pockets and he bounces on the balls of his feet.

"Excuse me?" I ask.

"No, I mean your shirt." He nods in my direction. "I'm a massive fan."

"Okay," I answer, "cool."

"In fact I named my dog after Kenny Rogers."

"What?"

"Kenny Rogers. I mean, 'The Gambler' seriously has to be one of the best songs ever recorded."

"Right," I say, looking down at the face on my shirt. "'The Gambler,' yeah, I agree for sure."

"Agree with what?" asks Grace, joining the conversation. She's nibbling on a toasted bagel. Where did she get that?

"We're just talking music over here," he says.

"We're both into similar stuff," I add.

"What stuff?" Grace sounds confused.

"We both love Kenny Rogers — you know, 'The Gambler.'"

"I didn't know you're a Kenny Rogers fan," she says to me.

"What? You didn't? Course I am, big time. Huge."

"I figured you guys would get along," says Grace. "I'm sure you have other shared interests."

"No doubt," I say, swallowing a yawn.

We continue talking, solely about Kenny Rogers, until Grace nods, telling me it's time. I follow her to the classroom, wiping my sweaty palms on the legs of my pants.

Hour One: Getting to Know You

Grace greets each student as they arrive and ushers them to a large green mat. I'm slouched at the blackboard, hands in my pockets. The entire class of thirty sits cross-legged around an empty wooden stool. Two of the youngsters furtively stick out their tongues at me. I return their salute. Grace guides me to the stool with her hand on my back. She tells the class I am her nephew and that if they have any questions, now is the time to ask. She retreats to her desk.

I seat myself on the stool. I fold my arms uncomfortably over my stomach and smile sheepishly at the back wall. I'm faced with a sea of waving hands. The first boy I call on slowly drops his arm when I point in his direction. He looks from right to left and after a few seconds just shrugs his shoulders.

The second child, an unsolicited girl with a frizzy ponytail, stands to announce in an unexpectedly emphatic voice, "You smell like coffee." She goes on to explain how her parents don't drink coffee anymore, only green tea. I want to tell her she looks like an owl, but instead I just say, "Okay, guys, I think this is the question circle, not the comment circle."

A red-haired boy with freckles is next. Finally, an appropriate question: he asks me my age. I let them guess. First I hear twenty-five. "Older," I say. The next guess, eighty. More questions follow, mostly regarding my gross beard and crooked teeth.

After question period the kids sit at their desks and draw. Some use crayons, others markers. I manoeuvre among the tables and chairs, examining the artwork enviously, handing out little sticky stars.

I stop at the desk of one girl who's dressed in a pair of jean overalls and white running shoes. She's biting her tongue in concentration. She's using a brown crayon and is clearly drawing some type of tree, a seemingly decayed weeping willow, blowing in a windswept meadow. The tree looks lonely, sad. Its tragic beauty holds my attention but is ultimately unbecoming, almost lurid. The more I examine it, the more it revolts me.

"I'm drawing you," she asserts, sensing my presence without taking her eyes off her picture.

"Excellent," I say, handing her a shiny red star.

Hour Two: Gym Class

I'm guiding a single-file line of about fifteen enterprising boys. The elementary school gym seems much smaller than I remember. When I was in school, it seemed so expansive.

Apart from its diminished size, everything else is identi-
cal. The climbing ropes hanging from the ceiling are the
same; so are the basketball nets with wooden backboards
painted white and the yellow overhead lights, which buzz
softly in the background. Even the scent of rubber balls
and sweat is familiar.

I let the boys decide which game they want to play.
I hope for dodge ball, but the group settles unreliably on
floor hockey. I realize afterwards that they would have vot-
ed for whatever game I said first.

One child, a plump, brash boy named Mitchell, crawls
over to the equipment room and screams. He knows the
parachute is in there and he wants to play with it. After much
cajoling I finally convince him to forget the parachute so we
can play hockey, but he has a condition — he demands to be
goalie. I'm hesitant. I find myself easily irritated by Mitchell and disinclined to grant him his wish. I think it started
when I heard him bragging to a girl in class that he had five
chocolate chip cookies in his lunch, and she couldn't have
any. She didn't seem to care, but I did. I love chocolate chip
cookies. I had visions of standing over Mitchell, slowly eating his cookies one by one as the crumbs rained down onto
his desk. But I give in. It takes ten minutes to strap him into
the goalie pads. "These smell," he says.

When the puck drops, I forget about Visitor's Day. I'm
not just supervising anymore; I'm back in gym class. I've
taken up a defence position on the red team, who were one
player short. I'm feeling good, feeling loose. I haven't played
a game of floor hockey in years. The plastic stick is too short
for me but my passes are crisp, my stick-handling has never

been so precise. And no one from the other team is getting by me — no one. I'm a wall of defence.

It's about fifteen minutes into the game, with our team ahead 1-0, when Mitchell starts voicing his complaints. "Iain," he's moaning. "Iain, I'm getting bored back here." His piercing voice sounds too old for a six-year-old. I think it's the way he pronounces his words. It takes Mitchell twice as long to say *bored* as it would any of the other kids. It's infuriating. I'm trying my best to ignore him. After all, we're in the middle of the game and I'm trying to win.

"It's okay, pal. Just hang in there."

"But no one's shooting on me."

"Yup, we're winning, champ. Let's try and remember that," I counter.

With Mitchell still lamenting his lack of action behind me, the pace of the game slows in front. Both teams are starting to float and lose interest. One group of boys is leaning on their sticks and chatting in a small circle. The game needs a spark.

I elegantly strip the puck from a boy in stocking feet (he forgot his gym shoes), dance around three opposing players, and from just a couple of steps in front of my own goal flip the puck high up off the gym floor. It moves purposefully through the air in what seems like slow motion and sails over the goalie's shoulder like a bird. The soft orange puck hits the very top right-hand corner of the net. *Goal!* — and what a beauty. The young blond goalie hasn't even moved; he's picking at the straps of his right pad.

I slap the blade of my stick on the floor. "Woooo!" I yell. "Brilliant! 2-0."

The gym is silent. I look around to see all the six-year-old boys staring blankly at me. Before I can speak, Mitchell pushes his goalie mask up over his head. "When we play hockey, the teachers aren't allowed to score," he declares, taking extra long to say *allowed*.

"Yeah," announces another boy, the one in stocking feet, "usually they don't even shoot."

"And I'm still getting no shots on me. I want some action!"

"Mitchell," I call over my shoulder, irritably, "I've been playing great defence — my job is to stop them from shooting on you. It's good for the team if you don't have to stop any shots. So just relax."

"More shots!" he demands.

We continue back and forth until Mitchell's voice grows ever louder and higher-pitched. I relent, and in the following minutes I allow any child with the puck clear access to our net. Mitchell is peppered with four shots, resulting in four goals. He's utterly helpless; it looks more like he is trying to avoid the puck than stop it.

"I hate being goalie," he declares. "I want to play defence."

"No, Mitchell, you asked to play goalie, and there isn't enough time left to switch the equipment."

I turn to run up the floor but Mitchell is sitting down now, refusing to play. Again I relent. It takes ten minutes to unbuckle Mitchell out of the bulky goalie pads. Just as I'm looking for his replacement, the bell rings and gym class is over. It's a flurry of yelling and irrepressible movement. Mitchell is first out the door, followed by the rest of the screaming kids. I'm left alone in the suddenly quiet gym with the discarded pads and an army of red and blue hockey sticks to collect.

Hour Three: Lunch

Before I leave I decide to stick around for lunch. Grace is headed for yard duty, so I stay inside to watch over the class. We sit and eat the lunches our parents have prepared. I'm hoping to convince one of the kids to trade for my bruised banana. I specifically asked Mom not to give it to me.

Most of the kids eagerly wolf down their meals and are outside within minutes. All except one boy, who is sitting alone at one of the miniature red tables. I walk over and sit down beside him. The boy, like me, is a slow eater. He's enjoying his food; each bite is chewed carefully and savoured. He's also shy and shows more concern for his carrot sticks than me. But after a few minutes he breaks the silence, leaning in close as if he has a secret to share. Raising his eyebrows, he delicately asks if I want to see the inside of his sandwich. When I say yes, he deliberately peels apart the two halves, revealing what appear to be slices of ham and cheese and strings of mustard and mayo. Wearing an expression that says, *Pretty crazy, isn't it?* he slaps his sandwich back together and takes a wee bite.

Back in my car I'm shivering, waiting for the engine to warm, reflecting on my morning. A charming end to my day back at school: this little boy, brimming with excitement and wonder at something as mundane and insignificant as a ham and cheese sandwich. It's a moment I can keep with me, a constant reminder of the innocence and general enthusiasm so many of us lack. I decide that this thoughtful boy, his ham sandwich, and all that it represents are the high-light of my morning.

Or at least it's a very close second. We're talking top corner here — the goalie never had a chance!

Twelve

A Bit of Sun

THE SNOW HAS FINALLY STARTED MELTING. We've been clustered in the kitchen all morning. I'm sitting on the counter eating a bowl of Mini-Wheats. Dad, a few feet to my right, sleeves rolled up, hunched over, is washing dishes in the sink. Mom's sleeves are also rolled up and she is drying with a blue and white tea towel. She stacks the bowls and plates before putting them away. They're working on the breakfast dishes but are focused on the sheep.

"I suppose about fifty percent of the time nothing bad happens."

"Yup, fifty percent sounds about right," echoes Mom.

I'm holding my bowl and spoon in one hand and draining the last of the milk directly into my mouth. "Okay," I sputter. "So then, fifty percent of the time something bad does happen."

"Yup, I'd say around fifty," says Mom.

"Give or take," agrees Dad.

They've been trying to have this talk with me for weeks,

the one about the dogs and cats and how to keep them fed and watered; the one about the sheep, explaining exactly how much hay to give them, when to give them stale bread, and how to lure them into the barn with a scoop of grain. They want to make sure I'm prepared for everything. Lambing season has arrived, bringing with it a handful of new arrivals. The last three of our Cheviot ewes are due this week.

The warmer weather has also induced a warmer mood. I find I'm in good spirits, my best in some time, and I've been looking forward to this week: the quiet, the solitude, the lack of human presence. I've decided I'm not going to leave Lilac Hill for the next three days. Not once. And I'm looking forward to it. I have everything I need here.

Tomorrow my parents are headed south, to Georgia. They're off to a conference where Dad will deliver a paper on eighteenth-century poetry. I've heard him reading it aloud to Mom for the past couple of days. He always gets her to edit his papers before these conferences.

I've been feeling unapologetically productive. I've been spending the majority of my time writing, often for several hours at a time. When I got into a groove like this in Toronto, I always felt guilty, as if I should be doing something else, something that would help pay the rent. But I've been living an inexpensive life and haven't felt that nip of guilt. I'm also feeling less confined, less anxious about still living with Mom and Dad. Maybe it's because I've been able to write more or because the cold has left. I'm not sure. But the lures of city life have been melting away with the ice and snow.

I brought up my living situation with Dad a couple of weeks earlier, as we stacked the last of the firewood. He was quick to brush the topic aside with a casual wave of his hand, the way he always has since I've returned. "It's okay; we're not too concerned about it. It'll be great if you're still here in a couple of weeks, when we go away. We'll need someone here to look after the animals, and it seems like you're doing a lot of writing, which is good." We stacked the rest of the wood in silence.

Even just four days alone at the farm will be a treat. Birthing mishaps are my sole concern. I've never been alone at the farm during lambing season before.

"Well, you can have a breech birth; they can get pretty tricky and are fairly common," says Dad.

"Yes, and sometimes the little hooves get stuck," continues Mom. She's dropped her towel on the counter in a damp ball and is demonstrating with her hands how the hooves can get wedged under the chin. "Just like this. Then you have to get your hands in there and help it through."

"In there?"

"Right, up in the birth canal."

"That's usually your mom's job because of her small hands."

Mom and Dad each hold up a hand as an offering of evidence. Dad's are three times as large. I jump down off the counter.

"What else?"

"Well, if you think the ewe is prolapsing or she isn't moving around but just lying there or foaming at the mouth, you can always call the vet."

"Or call a neighbour."

"Or call your brother."

This is their strongest point. If something goes wrong with the sheep or the cats or the dogs or, well, anything, I shouldn't try to figure it out. I should call others for help.

"Okay," I say, sliding my empty bowl into the sink. "I'll keep that in mind."

As I leave the kitchen, Mom's muttering something about Grandma being another good contact option. Just in case I need help. Grandma is ninety-one.

An hour or so later Dad's upstairs packing. Mom and I are reviewing more instructions. We've left the sheep, chickens, and ducks for the domesticated animals. None of the dogs or cats is pregnant, so I'm anticipating minimal theatrics. Mom's given me a clipboard, a blank sheet of paper, and a blue pen. She insists I take notes. I'm a couple of steps behind her as she prepares the dogs' dinners.

"Titan gets three of the big scoops. But one of the scoops comes from the blue bin. That's his special food."

"Why's it special?"

"It's dental dog food. He has a legitimate tartar problem."

"I was unaware. Go on."

"Now, as for Meggers, she gets only two scoops. Use the smaller scoop and get hers from the red bin. It's special diet food."

"Meg's on a diet?"

"Yes, her little hips are getting really sore, so we switched her onto the diet food. It's made a difference. She was getting pretty chubby there for a while."

"But don't you always give her treats after dinner?"

"Yes, but only one, or one and a half if it's a cold night."
Mom stands looking at Meg, who stares back, anticipating
her supper. "Well, sometimes maybe two."

I scribble down one and a half on a cold night, maybe
two. We move back into the house. I'm balancing the bowls
in one hand, and I lay them carefully down in front of the
heating vent on the kitchen floor. I've seen Mom put them
here to warm the food and the bowls. Mom is opening a can
of wet food.

"Now," she says, "you also have to break open one of
these glucosamine pills and empty it onto Meg's dinner.
That's also for those stiff hips."

This too goes down on the pad.

"Okay, she also gets two of these little pink pills, which
I just mix into some of this meat." Mom answers me before
I have time to ask. "They're for her thyroid."

Two pink thyroid pills, mix into meat. My page is filling up. I watch Mom take bits of meat and mix it into the
dry food with a fork. She does it methodically, tiny bits at a
time, to ensure that the meat mixes evenly with the kibble.

"As for ratios, since Meg is so much smaller I give her
a lot less."

"Makes sense."

"She usually gets around an eighth of a can or so, and
only at dinner. She doesn't need meat at breakfast unless it's
really cold or rainy, then you can put a little treat on her meal.
She's not picky; she'll eat anything leftover from your supper.
Cheese is good. Sometimes I sprinkle a little Parmesan on
there, or you could fry an egg quickly."

My head is down and I'm scribbling frantically.

"Obviously Titan gets a bit more; I usually give him almost the rest of half the can. So I guess about seven-eighths or so . . . of half."

The dogs attack their meticulously prepared meals, their metal collars clinking on their bowls. It has taken Mom much longer to assemble them than it does for Meg and Titan to inhale them. She continues with her hints as they occur to her. Titan loves rice. Meg loves chicken skin, so if I roast a chicken or a turkey I should save the skin for Meg. I hadn't planned on roasting any poultry while they're gone, but I suppose it's better to be safe than sorry. I jot down *Meg = chicken skin*.

The cats are up next. I observe Mom beckoning them affectionately in a high-pitched voice. She taps one of their tiny china dishes with a fork. This peculiar ritual works. The cats sprint into the kitchen in a blur of black, white, and orange fur.

My only concern about the cats is when I'm told about the shots of insulin that come with each feeding. Pumpkin, the old tabby, has developed diabetes. He's lived in the barn for most of his life. He's excruciatingly timid and is comfortable only around Mom. He often bolts under the furniture whenever Dad or I enter the room. Petting him will be a challenge for me, let alone injecting his back with shots of insulin twice a day.

"You shouldn't have a problem. Just wait till he's eating, then lightly pinch some of his loose skin and get the tip of the needle in there, and he won't even notice." As Mom explains the procedure, I'm peering at Pumpkin. He returns my skeptical gaze. "But be gentle. Your Dad's obviously my human soulmate, but Pumpkin, he's my feline soulmate."

With everyone fed and the medications put away, Mom steps into the living room, where Titan is savouring his post-supper nap. He's flaked out on his blanket, the tip of his pink tongue protruding from the edge of his mouth. His eyes are closed. Mom slowly bends down to her knees.

"If you rub just the right spot of his back or belly, right around here, and then stop, he'll actually give you a big smile. Won't you, boy? Yes, you will." She's scratching Titan's furry back with both hands like a masseuse. He stretches out his hind legs. Then she stops suddenly. Titan tilts his head lazily in her direction. "Oh, come on, Titan, don't you want me to keep going? Give me a smile."

He gapes at her and lets his head flop back down on the mat.

"I guess it's because you're here," says Mom, disconcertedly. "Hopefully he'll smile for you when you're alone. I swear it'll work after you feed him."

I nod but omit these last few instructions from the list. I leave Mom lying on the floor beside Titan, still working for a smile.

I don't see Mom again until she pops her head into my room. It's late. I'm reading in bed.

"I just want to let you know, you shouldn't use the upstairs toilet while we're gone."

"What do you mean? It was working fine an hour ago."

"I know, but I just remembered to clean it before bed so it would be nice and fresh for you, but I'm tired and

I accidentally flushed the rag down the toilet. I think it's stuck somewhere."

"You flushed the rag down the toilet . . . while you were cleaning it?"

"Uh-huh."

"How did you do that?"

"Good question. I'm not entirely sure either. But it happened somehow. Anyway, I'll let you sleep. Nighty-night."

I should take the time to find my list of instructions. Remembering not to use the upstairs toilet because Mom has lost a rag down the pipe is important. But when I overhear her waking Dad to tell him the same mystifying news, I'm confident that, after reviewing the event for the second time — and likely a third time in the morning when Dad tells me again at breakfast — copying it onto my list would be just plain gratuitous.

Ten minutes later I'm asleep. Another knock on the door wakes me.

"Oh, sorry, Iain." Mom opens the door a crack and again pokes her head in. "I was lying in bed and just remembered there's one more thing I want to tell you."

"Shoot," I sputter, lying flat on my stomach.

"I'm not sure if you know, but I've made a little bed for Pumpkin above Titan's doghouse. I used some old carpet and a fluffy towel. And I've been trying for weeks to get him to feel comfortable and sleep there. He was finally starting to get used it. I've been feeding him and giving him his shot there every morning. It's actually quite cute because —"

"Mom, is this just an adorable fable or do I need to know something?"

"Right, sorry. Well, yesterday and today I found a single egg in Pumpkin's bed and no Pumpkin. It's so frustrating. I guess one of the chickens has found the bed and is laying its eggs in there. It's spooked Pumpkin, though. So please just try and keep your eye on the situation because I don't want to be worrying about Pumpkin while I'm away."

"Done."

"It's so annoying because he was getting so used to sleeping there and it was warm and I wasn't worrying about him trying to find somewhere to sleep and —"

"*Okay.* Thanks, Mom," I sigh. "Night."

"Oh, right. Nighty-night."

The next morning is steeped in tension. It always is the morning of a trip. Mom and Dad rush around the house packing last-minute things, watering neglected plants, changing soiled litter boxes, polishing scuffed shoes. Dad also takes a few minutes, the way he always does before a trip, to say goodbye to the sheep in the barn. Mom uses that time to tell her favourite plants how healthy they are, touching their leaves and branches, telling them she'll be back soon.

After packing their bags into the trunk, Mom and Dad bid a final adieu to the cats and dogs, each receiving a pat and a personalized message. As we start down the lane I'm startled when Dad, buckled into the passenger seat, turns and asks me to stop the car. I slam on the brakes. Once we're in, he never wants to stop the car on the way to the airport. He'd be content to arrive there a couple of days before departure, just to be safe.

"Hold on a minute," he says, ducking out of the car door.

"What did you forget?"

But he's out before he can answer. I watch him in the rear-view mirror walking back towards the house. He steps softly, as if he doesn't want to wake the apple trees.

"Maybe he dropped something on the driveway," says Mom. "By the way, I read that the rain's supposed to continue all week; the umbrellas are by the side door if you need one. I even dug out the more masculine one for you, so it's there as well."

"I thought so," Dad announces, stepping back into the car, fastening his seatbelt. "The red-winged blackbirds have arrived. First time I've seen them this year. There were about four of them by the hanging feeders." He removes his glasses and wipes off the rain with his shirt.

"That's so exciting," says Mom, turning in her seat. "I knew I could hear more birds this morning."

As we drive away I'm adjusting the radio, hoping to find some traffic reports. Dad turns, pointing back at the house and the birds. Mom joins him, on her knees, peering out of the window.

When I return from the airport, the house is still and quiet. All the animals, even the cats, are outside. A nice book seems appropriate. I doubt you could find more suitable conditions for reading. I hope to do a lot of it. I discover that Dad has set one aside for me; he's left it by my computer. It's E. B. White's collection of essays, *One Man's Meat*. I take it to the living room and lie down on the couch, my head resting on a pillow. Dad's stuck a note to the cover: *Was going to take this on the plane, but Mom and I thought you might like it.*

I open it to the page he's marked. The essay is entitled "Spring." It comes with a subheading: "Notes on springtime and on anything else of an intoxicating nature that comes to mind." It was written in April 1941.

Considering the dramatic shifts of the past seventy-plus years and the ways in which the world has changed, I wonder how many notes regarding daily life written in the spring of 1941 will still be relevant today. I'm able to read only a couple of pages before my eyelids start to slip shut. It was an early morning, and these conditions are also pretty good for napping. But the last lines I read before my eyes close are released from the page, swimming around in my thoughts untethered, until I fall asleep: *The day of days when spring at last holds up her face to be kissed, deliberate and unabashed. On that day no wind blows either in the hills or in the mind, no chill finds the bone. It is a day that can come only in a northern climate, where there has been a long background of frigidity, a long deficiency of sun.*

The next morning is bright and warm. I'm up earlier than usual. My first task is to open a few of the windows that have been shut tight all winter. After my breakfast of scrambled eggs and toast, I'm sweeping up some dog fur when I spot the umbrellas hanging by the door. I won't need one today. The rain has left overnight. One is slightly larger and has a blue background with yellow stars. The other is smaller, compact; it's maroon with varying breeds of horses and ponies printed on the nylon. I can't be sure which one Mom has left specifically for me — neither screams masculinity. I grab my wool jacket from underneath the blue umbrella and step into my rubber boots.

Dad was right. The birds are back. This morning it's not just the red-winged blackbirds that are out but also the finches, chickadees, and blue jays, among others I don't recognize. They've gathered at Dad's hanging feeders in droves and are singing louder than I remember.

The ground is soft, clay-like, and squishes under my boots. The careless snow has left behind puddles freckled across the yard. The grass is yellow and fledgling. Spring has made smells relevant again. Here at the farm smells become pungent and stale in the heat of the summer, fade with the light in autumn, and are made sterile in the frozen temperatures of winter. They are reborn in spring. I'm immediately presented with a rich cast of scents to choose from, some more appealing than others. The chicken coop, for example, offers an aroma that is equal in strength and vileness. I pull up my jacket over my nose and stay just long enough to collect the freshly laid eggs and pass along my cordial regards to the hens.

I bring the eggs inside for a wash. I'm followed by Titan, who's followed by Pumpkin. We are a three-creature train. Once inside they flop down together, only inches apart, on Titan's blanket. Pumpkin purrs his gravelly, laborious purr. Titan exhales lavishly through his nose. Mom swears that the two ageing animals are best friends and that Pumpkin won't sleep out in the open unless Titan is close by. She says that Pumpkin will sit and meow by the front door if Titan is waiting there, until someone lets his mate in.

They aren't just lying together now. Pumpkin is spooning his much larger pal.

All day I've been finding notes from Mom around the house. Most I skim once, maybe twice, if only to ensure that I understand her thought. But I find one in the fridge worth reading over a few times. It's stuck to the front of the cheese keeper. *Try not to give Pumpkin any of the Danish blue or Stilton cheese . . . Both give him awful gas.* I appreciate how she wrote *try.* The temptation just might be too strong.

Another reminds me that there is a full tank of propane on the barbecue and to use up any of the meat in the freezer. This seems like a good idea. The afternoon has kept the morning's promise of sun and warmth. I head out to the verandah with a couple of frozen sausages and my book. I don't just cook on the verandah but stay outside to eat. Afterwards I read in my chair until it gets too dark to see.

Again I wake early from a restful sleep. I carry two buckets of water out to the barn for the sheep. There won't be many days left of carrying water; it will soon be warm enough to set up the automatic watering system again. A quick head count reveals that one ewe is missing. I find her in the neighbouring barn. She is lying on the ground, exhausted. Beside her is a single lamb.

The lamb is tiny, wet, and shivering. I take a handful of straw and rub along its rib cage and limbs to dry its body and increase circulation. The mother gradually stands and stomps the ground forcefully, telling me she's got it under control. I drop the straw and step back but continue to watch. The ewe moves in and nudges the lamb with her head, encouraging it to stand. The lamb's legs look two sizes too big for its body. It takes a few tries before it can successfully get on its feet. Once it does, walking doesn't seem so hard, and the lamb stumbles around the pen, searching instinctually for its mother's teat, its long tail wagging furiously.

The rest of the flock are unconcerned about the new arrival. They're hungry, waiting for breakfast. I fill the metal feeder with their morning provender. They eagerly gather around my legs, pushing to get closer. I cut the twine and take a few minutes to break up the hay. The lambs that were born earlier are still too young to eat hay. They circle the adults, gambolling about. They're young children chasing one another at a family barbecue, running around the picnic table. They run and jump just for the sake of running and jumping; they have energy to burn. It won't last much longer, maybe another couple of weeks. The oldest lamb, the one with tiny horns sprouting above his ears, has already outgrown this playful activity and has joined the others pushing about at the feeder. He's not eating the hay but stands alongside the older sheep.

It's now, watching the sheep eat, that I recall for the first time a chat I had with my friend Bob in Toronto. It happened right around this time of year. He was telling me that spring doesn't exist anymore, at least not as a distinct season. "It's just a few weeks of rain while everyone looks forward to summer."

Bob is right. I spent the last four years in the city, where spring has lost much of its authority and has been relegated to a backup role, meant only to shepherd winter out through the front door and hold it open for summer. But spring is still a legitimate season at the farm.

From the barn I stroll across the field to the duck pen. I have some bread for the ducks and stale crackers for the chickens and Lucius, if he's around. The ducks emerge in ordered panic, quacking, waddling out of their hut with renewed interest in the yard. They find the muddy puddle water instantly and dive in like the first beachgoers of the year. I bet the ducks would have left their feathery coats hanging inside if they could. It's still too cold for the unadventurous hens, though. They'll wait for another few weeks before venturing out of the coop to dig around in the muck, hoping to unearth unsuspecting worms and bugs. I toss them their crackers along with an apple core for dessert.

I am outside tucking into my own lunch, a tomato and cheese sandwich. Again the rain has stayed away. I haven't had to call anyone for assistance, not the vet or a neighbour or my brother. Not even Grandma. Nor have I received any calls; no one asking how I'm doing or what I've been up to, or if I'm short on money, or if I'm feeling guilty about not working, or if I'm looking for a new job yet, or how I can possibly fill whole days alone at the farm, or why my beard is so long. Apart from pleading with Pumpkin, trying to convince him that we're out of Danish blue as he stands meowing at the fridge, I've barely spoken in three days.

I've brought a can of beer outside with me. Dad stocked

up Little Blue before they left. It might be a little early, I know, but with the sheep enjoying their hay and the ducks making use of the muddy water, I'm inclined to join in. I lean back, resting my head against the wall of the shed, and crack my beer open. Today's the first day I haven't worn my coat outside.

I will be picking up Mom and Dad early tomorrow morning. Their flight lands sometime around 9 a.m. But for now, I'm still alone. Alone but not lonely. Directly to my left, Titan and Pumpkin are locked in a lazy horizontal embrace. To my right, Lucius, who has been hidden for most of the winter, is pecking around in the dirt, chirping his brassy chirp. I'm again taken aback by his sharp features. My God, he's a revolting creature. But I don't shoo him away as I would have last summer. He might as well stay.

I'm sitting on the wooden stoop under the clothesline, facing the sun, sipping my beer. I can see one of the other cats, I think Harry Snugs or maybe Little Miss, strutting across the metal roof of the barn. When I finish this one, I'll go back inside for another and drink it here, where I drank my first.

Thirteen

Catching Up

IT's JUST AFTER 8 A.M., EARLY, I know, to be eating sardines directly from the can. I'm using a plastic straw as a one-pronged fork. I was lured to the kitchen the way I usually am, by the promise of coffee. I drank a cup while flinging open the cupboards and fridge, seeking out a pairing for my drink. I had plenty of options — fruit, cereal, toast — but I felt like trying something different, something offbeat, and went for the canned sardines instead. As soon as I pried open the can and saw those little heads and tails crowded together in a row, I regretted my decision. There's a reason toast and cereal are mainstays of breakfast. I straggle into the living room, fish in hand, in search of the paper.

"Don't distract me; I'm writing a letter." Mom's parked at the table, still wearing her slippers and pyjamas. Her short hair is askew, cowlicked on both side and back. Layers of sticky notes, cards, and envelopes are laid out in front of her like a paper feast. Her computer is open. "I've been meaning to write it for weeks. It's a thank-you letter and needs to be sent today. Dad said he'd mail it for me as soon as I finish." She pauses for a dramatic sip of her coffee. "It should have been done weeks ago. And now I'm stuck."

"What are you stuck on?"

"I'm trying to word a section about what you've been up to."

"What? Why am I showing up in your thank-you letter?'

"It's also a catch-up letter."

"But surely you can leave me out."

"I honestly don't mind putting you in."

"No, seriously, I'm happier to be left out. Just drop me, move on to the next section."

From somewhere in his study, Dad clears his throat. "If I'm in the letter, then Iain should be too."

"That's what I'm saying," agrees Mom, sounding vindicated. She starts drumming her pencil on the table.

"That's not true! No one needs to be caught up on me. There's nothing to be caught up on."

"Sure there is. You've been back home for a year now."

"Exactly."

"I just have to figure out how to word it."

"You'll figure it out; you always do," calls Dad. "Iain, let your mom write her own letter."

I settle down on the couch, opening the front section of the paper before my face like a screen.

But the sight and scent of my unconventional breakfast is too unsettling for Mom. She peers up from her notes anxiously. "What kind of breakfast is that? There's plenty of eggs and fresh bread in the kitchen."

"I know, but I didn't feel like cooking. I'm fine."

"But your dad picked about a dozen fresh eggs from the coop this morning."

"I just wanted something quick and easy. This is fine. I'm happy."

I rarely hear Dad snort, but he does now from his study. "Eggs are quick and easy, and very good for you."

"Also, you love them. You always have," says Mom, setting her pencil down.

"I know, but —"

"I can remember when you used to eat four or five in one sitting." Dad sounds completely ambushed. "It was amazing."

"You would eat them fried or scrambled or poached . . . you just loved them."

"I still like eggs, guys, but I don't crave them as much since I've been back home. Probably 'cause they're so readily available."

"Did you hear that?" Mom calls to Dad. "Iain's off eggs."

I hear Dad's chair push back against his bookcase as he rises from his desk. This startling news has roped him in from the study. He arrives with a puzzled look on his face. "But Iain loves eggs."

"I know," says Mom. "And ours are so fresh and delicious. Not to mention organic."

I've discovered the problem with impaling the sardines with the hollow straw is that with each piece, several drops of the fishy oil unavoidably collect in the tip, creating an unappealing mouthful. I don't mind the fish but loathe their unctuous bathwater. I'm in mid-chew, delaying the next bite, when a balled-up piece of loose-leaf hits my forehead.

"Wait. What have you done? You look different," exclaims Mom, who's standing now.

"I bet it's connected to this whole egg thing," says Dad.

"Maybe, but take a look for yourself. He definitely looks different today."

They move in closer, eyeballing me with stern resolve. I put my half-eaten meal down on the armrest and grin. It's taken a little longer than I'd thought. Before my kitchen stop I'd just come from the bathroom, where I'd shaved off my Karl Marx–style beard, right down to the wood. It's left my face noticeably puffy and red. I've worn beards of varying lengths ever since I returned home last year, but the most recent beard had been growing, unguarded, for months. It was shaggy and unkempt. I haven't been clean-shaven in well over a year. I look about ten years younger.

"You might be right," says Dad. "He looks cleaner. Did you bathe this morning?"

"Bathe? No, I didn't bathe, Dad."

"He's right though, Iain. You do look cleaner."

"I still think it has to do with the eggs," says Dad determinedly.

I wonder what they would say if my eight-year-old self, all four feet and sixty pounds of him, strolled into the living room tomorrow morning eating a can of sardines.

Did you do something different?

Who, me?

Yeah, something's not quite the same.

What do you mean?

I'm not sure, but you look more innocent this morning, or something.

Dad would have his own take. *Or maybe a little more optimistic — new trousers, bud?*

Mom returns to her seat at the table. Dad stares for a breath longer. "I know! Did you shampoo your hair?" he asks.

I shake my head.

"Could just be our imaginations, then."

Again I shake my head, but Dad's already retreated back to his study.

"Add that to your letter, Mom," I suggest. "That Iain's looking cleaner and shampooing his hair now, which is good news, but you're still a tad concerned since he's stopped eating eggs."

Mom's quick to disregard my suggestion. "Now you're just being silly."

It's getting close to lunch when I pass through the living room again. I'm en route to the kitchen but hesitate in front of the closet. I detect some rustling. It's probably a cat tunnelling around in one of the parkas. I'm about to investigate when Mom emerges, backing out slowly on her knees. She's wearing a brown fur coat. There's a patch of fur missing from the collar and one of the buttons is missing.

"What do you think?" she asks, standing slowly. "Your aunt Charlotte gave me this coat and I've never worn it. I just found it when I was putting some shoes away."

"When did she give it you?"

"I'm not sure . . . maybe ten or twenty years ago."

If possible, the coat would cough a few times, hack up some yellow phlegm onto the carpet, smear on a thick hoop of bright red lipstick, and, with a smutty wink, reveal her age to be closer to forty .

"Are you sure it's only twenty years old?"

"I'm sure it's much older than that; it wasn't new when she gave it to me. It was a hand-me-down." Shocking.

"I don't know, Mom; it's not really fur-coat weather these days. It's almost summer."

"I know, and I don't usually like fur coats at the best of times, but I've just had this one for so long." Her tone implies a deep sentimental attachment. I've never seen her wear this ghastly pelt.

"How often do you wear it, Mom?"

"You mean wear it out? Oh, never. I've never worn it. I had totally forgotten about it until just now." She moves in front of the large mirror mounted on the wall and faces her reflection. She slowly turns to her left, maintaining eye contact with her fuzzy profile. "Doesn't mean I can't start."

"It looks a little small — the sleeves don't even reach your wrists."

"It's a three-quarters cut; that's how it's meant to be. Actually this one's a tad big." She turns to the other side. "Maybe you're right; I don't think I can wear it. I look like a little brown bear."

"Actually, yeah, a little . . ."

"Well, what do you think about getting my hair cut, only this time I leave half untouched and cut the other half really short? My haircuts are always so symmetrical."

"I think most cuts are typically symmetrical."

"That's boring. Any second thoughts about the coat?"

"It's hard to get a sense, since you're still in your pyjamas."

"You're right, it's ridiculous. I was going to go up and get changed hours ago."

"How's the letter coming?"

"It's coming, but I got a little sidetracked."

When I walk through the dining room forty minutes later, Mom's still wearing the coat. She's settled on the floor now, her back resting against the stool. An old black photo album is open across her lap.

"I know, I know," she says. "I went to find a ruler in the drawer and came across this damn album. Now I can't put it down."

She ponders each picture intently. She waves me over to see a few. There doesn't appear to be any order or pattern. Some are from the farm in Oxfordshire where Mom and Dad rented a cottage after they were married, some are from dinner parties with friends in Canada, a few are from their actual wedding day. I'm pretty sure I recognize the fur coat in one picture. It's being worn by an elderly lady standing beside an elderly man I've never seen before. I don't mention anything to Mom.

"I can't believe it's been almost a year since I moved home," I say, sitting down on the stool, resting my chin in my hands, my elbows on my knees.

"What?" Mom peers up from the pictures.

"Nothing. I've just been thinking about this last year and being back at the farm."

"Oh, yeah."

For a few minutes, neither of us speaks.

"It's just funny how things play out," I say.

"Yup, and I think life's better when it's unpredictable."

"It's kind of hard to believe, but I feel like it's done me some good, you know."

"We hoped it would," she says.

Mom refocuses on her album, lingering on each page, pointing out how young everyone looks. "Especially Dad and I. We look ancient now compared to this."

One picture in particular has piqued her interest. She lifts the book higher for me to see. It's a picture of Dad standing outside the dairy cottage, dressed in wellington boots, a tweed jacket, and a scarf. He's holding a leather briefcase at his side. "I remember I took this one morning before your Dad walked to work. Most mornings he would walk across the field to catch a train. I've been pretty lucky," she says. "Still am."

I watch her peel back the thin plastic barrier and remove the photo from the book without explanation. She's mumbling to herself as she walks into the kitchen. It takes her a minute or two but she's able to shift around a few other pictures to free up a small gap on the top left corner of the fridge door. She sticks the newly recovered photo there, of Dad in his wellington boots, with a yellow and black magnet shaped like a bumblebee.

The afternoon has turned warm, even for May. On my last trip through the living room, Mom's papers were still littered across the table, but she was absent. I called a few times, but when no one answered, I wandered outside.

I stroll around the back of the house without a destination in mind. Meg's asleep beside one of the rock gardens. I walk quietly past her to Dad's magnolia tree. It hasn't changed much. Somehow Meg detects my soft steps and is up instantly, investigating the nascent tree along with me. The tree has stayed consistently unremarkable — short, frail, and sparse. There is only one appreciable change since I've last seen it: green buds have sprouted at the ends of each branch. I don't know enough about botany to know if these buds indicate that the tree is doing well or still struggling. The green buds are small and untrustworthy. There are no blooms, no flowers. The tree looks thirsty. I bend down and feel the earth around the base of the tree. I've seen Dad watering its roots every day for the past week, and this afternoon the dark soil feels gluey and damp. Mom must have been out yesterday adding some compost to its base. She's mixed it into the soil unscientifically. I walk on. Meg retreats, hoping to find that her spot by the garden is still warm.

"Where's Mom?" I've spotted Dad in the stone shed. He's wearing work gloves and a red baseball cap stained with dots of white paint. "Did she finish her letter?"

"No, not yet. She's upstairs on the phone. She forgot, said she's been meaning to catch up on some calls for a couple of days."

"Amazing."

"Are you busy? I could use a hand."

Mom's been after Dad for weeks to clean out the shed. Since she's taking care of some of her own chores today, Dad elected to do the same. He does it each year, between spring and summer. It's not a job he relishes. And the shed never looks any different. It's eternally filled with an impressive collection of unimpressive stuff, mostly old, broken, or damaged stuff. It's all worthless. Some will eventually escape outside, to the chicken run. That's the typical lifespan of my parents' belongings. The chicken run is the cemetery where most of their stuff is laid to rest after spending years deteriorating in the shed. Dad has the old basketball backboard, a box air conditioner, and a cracked satellite dish propped up against weathered two-by-fours in the chicken run. "It gives the hens some extra shade," he claims.

I tell Dad I'm not busy and he tosses me a pair of gloves. We toil mostly in silence. I lose track of time, but several feet outside the shed we've mobilized a small army of junk on the grass.

"Should I go grab some garbage bags?" I notice Dad has brought only one black garbage bag with him. It's sticking out of his back pocket. There's enough debris here to fill five or six. It's as if he's brought a thimble to empty a bathtub.

"Well, hold off, we should go through this stuff first. Probably don't want to throw it *all* away."

We start sifting through the insipid collection. Dad's save pile is growing at an alarming rate. He finds varying levels of value in the majority of our haul. I hold them up, hoping he's going to give me the nod when I uncover a pair of children's cross-country ski boots from the late 1970s. But Dad squints fondly at the boots and says, "Oh yeah, I forgot about those." He drops a rusty metal fan he's holding and steps towards me, taking a boot in his hand. "Those were your Mom's. You wouldn't remember, but we used to ski a lot more when we first moved out here. We would just go straight back for miles." I know Mom's never going to use her old boots again. I also know there's no way Dad's going to get rid of them. "May as well hang on to those. I think I can find a place for them in the rafters."

When the sorting is done, Dad removes his hat and gloves. He sits down on a squeaky aluminum lawn chair and hangs his hat over his knee. "I've been hearing that some of the land around here is going to be sold to developers. It's close enough to the city to start a small subdivision."

It's unexpected news. For a moment I consider the implications silently.

"You mean right around here?"

"Yup."

I did see a truck and what looked like a backhoe in one of the fields yesterday. There was a group of men milling about, but I didn't give it much thought.

"Is that what the digging was about yesterday?"

"I bet they were trying to find water reserves for wells," he says.

Dad points to the rolling field in front of us. In the distance is an old barn that used to hold dairy cattle. Like the fields, it's been empty for years. "Probably tear the old barn down, divide it up into two- or three-acre lots. It'll look a little different, won't it?"

"Yup," I say. "But I guess it's inevitable."

"I guess. You can't stunt progress."

"Nope."

"Things just keep moving forward."

"Have you told Mom yet?

"Not yet."

Dad stands and shakes out a faded canvas tarp that was folded in the shed. It's creased and dusty. Together we cover the pile of stuff we're keeping. We'll perform today's task in reverse and bring it all back into the shed tomorrow.

"I got an interesting email today," I say. It's not calculated; I didn't plan on saying anything, so I surprise myself.

"Regarding what?"

I tell Dad how I finally sent some of the writing I've been working on to a friend in Toronto, the only professional writer I know. He read it and replied, saying he liked it. He had passed it along to his editor and also gave me a list of names and contacts for literary agents. He said if I'm serious, that should be my next move: continue writing and try to find an agent.

"Brilliant. That's pretty exciting," says Dad. "What's involved in getting an agent?"

"I have no idea, really."

Dad's trying to scrape some dried mud off the tarp with a sharp stick but stops now to answer.

"Anyway, it's great news."

"Well, not much yet; just a couple of emails."

"It's great," he says.

"I've also been thinking, maybe it's time I should start looking for a place," I venture. "Nothing big or anything, but, you know . . ."

He's fiddling with the tarp again. "It's up to you."

I haven't done it in a long time, but suddenly I have the urge to shake Dad's hand or hug him or, I don't know . . . something.

"I was just telling Mom about — well, it seems like

my time here at the farm has been pretty beneficial." I stay standing where I am. "It has. I've been thinking about a lot of things and —"

"Well," he says, "this is a good place for thinking about things."

"Yeah."

He hands me a couple of logs. "Here, take these."

I lay them on my side of the tarp to hold it down like paperweights. The edited reject pile, now only two ripped feed bags, some frayed binder twine, and a ripped pillowcase hardened into a muddy mat, fits easily into the single garbage bag Dad brought with him.

"I know what it is! You shaved!"

I'm at the kitchen sink, my back aimed at my parents, filling a glass of water. Mom and Dad are sitting at the table. Neither can see my face. Dad's nibbling on some mixed nuts. Mom's moved her computer and papers into the kitchen. The letter is still incomplete.

"You're absolutely right, he did. It's so obvious now," says Dad.

"It's sooo obvious."

"It's pretty obvious," I answer, shaking my head.

"I can't believe I didn't realize it right away — you had that moustache for a while," says Mom.

"Moustache? No, Mom. I mean, I guess I did, but I had a full beard too. It was a beard."

"Really? I could have sworn you just had a big, fancy moustache."

"A moustache sounds vaguely familiar," admits Dad.

I close my eyes and drain my full glass of water. Immediately I start filling it again.

Dad pops a handful of nuts into his mouth. "Are you done yet? I better get up to the post office soon."

"I know, I know. I'm on the last paragraph. I just need some silence."

I grant Mom her silence by heading out to the porch. Every so often Dad asks if Mom's finished, because, he reminds her, the post office will be closed soon. She's not but is always close. One time she's on the last thought; the next time, the last sentence.

I hear some indecipherable whispering. Then Dad's chuckling, and Mom's laughing too. Finally Dad jogs past me with the letter in hand. He climbs into his truck and drives off to mail it. Even though her computer was on all day, she ended up writing the letter by hand. Mom sneezes a couple of times, shuts down her computer, packs up her papers, and heads upstairs to change out of her pyjamas.

I'm leaning in now, my hands on either side of the sink, my face an inch or so away from the mirror. I shaved just this morning, about ten hours ago; still, I lather a shot of blue shaving gel between my fingers and cover the lower half of my face.

I should go outside and take a walk. It's a nice evening. I can hear the kettle fussing from the kitchen. Mom will be making a pot of tea, probably chamomile. Dad's settled in for the evening; the playoff hockey game has been switched on down the hall.

Maybe I should give that fancy moustache a try. But if I want a moustache, does that mean I should just grow a beard again? Maybe I should stay clean-shaven for a while. But does it really matter? It starts growing again the second you shave it off. It never stops growing. It's growing again even *while* you shave it.

I walk over to the window and peer between the white slats of the blinds. It's a view I know well. I've stood contemplating this scene from the bathroom window hundreds of times growing up, and probably hundreds more this year. The evening sky is a blend of pink and red. There are a few thin clouds on the horizon, but mostly it's clear. I've seen this sky before too, with these same wispy clouds. If the land is developed, if homes are built as Dad thinks they will be, this view will be permanently altered; large houses, uniform backyards, and tall fences will replace the grass, dirt, and streams. Those fields will be hidden by advancement, by progress.

I can see Lucius now. He's emerged onto the middle of the barn's silver roof. He's holding his little head up and out, screeching towards the back fields. Tonight I sense a certain declaration of happiness in his squealing. The weather's changed; like the rest of us he's pleased to see spring. He's also clearly content with his choice of family. And why wouldn't he be? He's provided with shelter and food; he's encouraged, looked after, showered with attention, and loved unconditionally. For an eccentric guinea fowl, he's got it pretty good.

I move back to the sink and splash a few handfuls of water on my face, washing away the scented gel. I dry myself with the beige cotton towel hanging on the back of the door and rub my hand across my cheek. I can barely feel it but it's already there — the relentless, rebounding stubble.

I think I'll have some of that tea. I reckon Mom will have a few more pictures from her album to show me. And then I'll make some popcorn or have a big bowl of ice cream — I saw some in the freezer yesterday. And then maybe I'll take a book out to the verandah. Dad's plucked a Nancy Mitford novel out of his bookcase for me; it's one he thinks I'll "particularly enjoy." I could offer to barbecue supper. I wonder what we're having. Dishes will need to be washed and dried and put away. I should watch a period or two of the hockey game. There will be animals to feed, litter boxes to clean, and plants to water. I haven't seen much of the dogs today. Both are due for a pet.

But first I'd better take that walk.

Author's Note

SINCE THE COMPLETION OF THIS BOOK I've left Lilac Hill and moved into my own apartment. I returned to the farm for a few days last Christmas, with the more comfortable title of visitor. We had to set an extra seat at the table for my sister's second son. Well, metaphorically. He was only three months old at the time and mostly lay on the couch chewing his index finger. The only bit of sad news is the passing of Meg, our border collie, who died suddenly but painlessly in early December. Pumpkin the cat has shamelessly usurped her bed.

At Christmas dinner we listened to music, toasted, ate, and drank. We reminisced about the year I moved home and I told everyone about the book I'd written. I wasn't asked to whistle. Not once. Everything else at the farm was as I'd left it. Dad still fancies his magic cords, Mom's still allergic to her cellphone, and Lucius still waits stoically on the verandah for his morning meal. A modest housing development is planned for a neighbouring field. Construction has yet to start.

Some names were changed for the sake of anonymity. Excerpts from two chapters were originally broadcast on CBC Radio's *Out Front*.

Acknowledgements

I WOULD LIKE TO THANK MY SKILFUL EDITOR, Janie Yoon, and my esteemed agent, Samantha Haywood. Without them this book wouldn't be a book and I would still be licking honey off my shirt. I would also like to thank the Ontario Arts Council for its assistance.

I hold much gratitude for my small but supportive family (all of you at the Christmas table). I'm particularly indebted to my sister for all her help and keen eye for detail.

Also thanks to House of Anansi Press, CBC Ottawa, the country of Iceland, Ian Coutts, The Manx pub, the Victory Café, Catharine Lyons-King, Erin Lawson, Meg Masters, Stuart McLean, Alex Schultz, my friends, and, most imperatively, Lucius.

Thanks, Mom and Dad. I owe you one.

We all know writing is a reclusive, lonely endeavour. It just is. But nobody writes alone.